Chapter:

"Maybe you could put on a better show?" Aila asked as they were at the rear of the group.

"Better show of what? Eating? I'd just get it all over my bones and then in my boot! Ugh, boot dinner. I might be undead but I have standards!" Anthony tilted his head up to the sky, just in time to get hit by a low lying branch, knocking him backwards, only just able to stay in his seat as Tommie and the guide taking them to Selenus looked back.

"See, always remember to wear a helmet when riding, safety first! Anthony recovered.

Tommie sighed and the Elven Guide went back to ignoring them.

"Damn, did I dent it?" Anthony asked, touching his helmet.

"Just, try and be a bit more low-key could you? I'm pretty sure that the guide already thinks something is wrong with you. Death Knights aren't exactly welcomed company."

"I am an upstanding Death Knight!" Anthony sounded hurt.

A number of responses went through Aila's mind before she closed her mouth, unable to pick one.

It wasn't much longer that the forest was starting to thin out and more sunlight was getting through the canopy.

The guiding elf coughed as Aila looked up front where the tree line ended and a city could be seen in the distance.

"We've arrived at Enni. This is where I leave you," she said.

"Thank you for guiding us." Aila touched her head and saluted the elf.

"As is my duty." The elf responded with the same salute.

The guide turned and headed back into the forest as Aila got a closer look at the city Enni.

There was a wide variety of people of all different sizes working the fields that had to be two or three times the fields that circled Laisa.

"So this is a beast man town?" she asked.

1

"A lot of them are bigger than humans and the other races, and they require more food," Anthony said, noticing her looking at the fields.

"They're alchemists—should have the compound I require," Tommie said, looking at the town closer.

"Compound?"

"Oh, did I say that out loud?" Tommie just laughed awkwardly and then averted his eyes, not answering her question.

"Let me know when the Gnome-inator is done!" Anthony said.

"Of course! You gave me so many great ideas!" Tommie had a wide, almost crazed smile as he patted the burlap sack filled with parts and components. Aila, even with all of her studying, didn't know what they could possibly create.

"Come on then!" Anthony let out a high-pitched squeaking whistle. "Really isn't the same without lips."

Those in the nearby fields were looking over at them as they walked out of the tree line.

Anthony waved to them in greeting.

Aila, with her Far Sight, was able to see the panic on the farmer's faces when they saw the trio. One of them dropped to all fours and ran off through the fields, getting the attention of a wandering group of soldiers.

"Looks like we'll have company soon," Aila said.

The runner waved in their direction, talking to the soldiers. They followed the runner back at a jog, heading directly for them.

"I don't have a good feeling about this," Aila said in a singsong voice.

"I'm really close to the beast men. I had some really close beast men friends!" Anthony said.

Aila didn't feel any more confident with his words.

They continued forward and more patrols appeared. There was a group of beast men soldiers on the walls of the city as the farmers all moved back.

"Who fights today!" Anthony said when the group was in earshot.

The beast men all leveled their weapons with the group.

"Get off your beast and put down your weapons!" the leader yelled out.

"That went well," Aila said.

"I'm pretty sure that is the general greeting," Anthony said.

"Stop talking!" The leader gestured with his spear, as the tribal tattoos across his body started to surge with power. The other beast men also readied themselves for a fight.

"We're just passing through. We don't want any trouble." Anthony kept his hands up and visible.

"A human comes into beast man territory and they don't want trouble." One of the guards let out a snort and pawed the ground.

Guess he's got a rather lot of warthog heritage, Aila thought, looking at him.

"All humans have to be questioned and identified," the guard captain said. His eyes turned to Tommie and Aila.

"Okay, very well," Anthony said. He slowly got down from Ramona.

"Thank you for letting me borrow your mount," Anthony said, looking at Aila.

"No problem," Aila said.

What does he mean by that? She looked relaxed on the outside but inside felt he was plotting something.

The guards grabbed Anthony, putting manacles on his wrists and taking away his sword and scabbard. They removed his cloak, revealing his armor.

"A knight." The leader scoffed and turned his eyes to Tommie and Aila again.

"Get registered at the town gates." With that, he turned with the rest of the patrol and headed for the city, roughly dragging and pushing Anthony ahead of them.

"You'll scuff the armor!" Anthony complained.

They only started to do it more.

Why is he letting them push him around? Aila had an understanding of his strength and there was no way that those manacles or those beast men were stronger than Anthony.

"What do we do now?" Tommie asked, still looking scared from it all.

"I guess we get registered. Trust me, Anthony isn't in danger," Aila said.

Tommie took a few moments. "He's the strongest person I've ever met." Tommie nodded as he coaxed his mount forward.

"Come on, Ramona," Aila said.

The big beast looked at Aila with a pitiful look.

"He'll be fine," Aila said.

Ramona seemed to give in, lowering her head and following them.

***

Captain Etheras put down his report and pulled the glasses off his snout. "You captured a human who was travelling with a gnome and a dark elf, and you have been questioning him, but you haven't been able to take his armor. So you can't use the Eyes of Truth on him?" he asked Lieutenant Ralo.

"Yes, Captain." Ralo's ears tucked down and his tail didn't move under the captain's gaze.

Etheras was from the wolf clans and they had some links to the coyotes.

"What has he said?" Etheras asked.

"He said that he is only passing through. He is travelling to Ilsal," Ralo reported faithfully, relieved to have something that would put him in a good light and show he was at least *trying* to do his job.

"Does he have papers saying that he is an Ilsal citizen?"

"No."

"His weapons and armor?"

"He says that he won't take them off—he doesn't want to freak people out." Ralo frowned before he cleared his throat. "The armor is specially made. We haven't been able to pull it off, or even open the helmet so we can use the Eyes of Truth on him. I think that it might even be some kind of artifact. It has this tree on the back and it glows and moves. His sword we can't pull out of the scabbard but I got one of the smiths to examine it. He says he's never seen anything like it. He thinks that it is made from ores only found in the heart of dwarven lands. He even keeps on saying that he's saying the truth."

"What is the rule?"

"Never trust someone who has not been checked with the Eyes of Truth." Ralo stood straight and answered rapidly, the words burned into his mind.

Etheras tapped his glasses on the desk before he put them down. "Let's see just what he wants." He stood up.

"Sir?" Ralo asked.

"I have nothing but boring reports waiting for me, and it is not every day that we have a human on this side of the border," Etheras said, already walking for the door. "Are you coming?"

"Yes sir!" Ralo stumbled into action and followed him out across the training ground and into the heavy stone buildings that made up the city's jail.

No human would be able to break out of here. They're made to withstand even someone from the ox clan trying to break out.

Etheras wandered down into the depths of the jail, where he heard screeching and scratching.

"Ahhh!"

"Nooo!"

"What are you doing!" a man yelled.

But Etheras's ears perked up.

"Is he...*laughing?*" Etheras picked up the pace. He saw a man on a rack with three guards trying to lever off his armor as he laughed and bucked, clearly acting as if he were being tickled by them.

Etheras let out a growl.

The guards stopped what they were doing and looked at Etheras, saluting him awkwardly. One of them dropped their tool on their foot, wincing as they saluted while one eyebrow fluctuated wildly.

"At ease." Etheras moved in front of the man, who was starting to get himself back under control.

"Oh, sorry about the noise. Just, they wouldn't stop, you know," the man said, taking a few breaths.

"Who are you?" Etheras asked.

"Anthony. And you are?"

"Guard Captain Etheras. We need you to answer a few questions," Etheras said.

"Sure!"

"We need you to answer them while under the effect of the Eyes of Truth," Etheras said.

"Can you just put it up against my helmet and we do it that way?" Anthony asked.

"We need to make sure you're not using some kind of means to stop the spell from working."

"I would if I could, but I think you might get a bit freaked out," Anthony said.

"Freaked out." Etheras repeated the words, clearly not amused. "Look, I'm nearly eighty years old, so I've been fighting ever since the slaver wars."

"Slaver wars?" Anthony asked.

"Humans forget so soon," Ralo said.

Etheras glanced at him, making Ralo stand straight and close his mouth.

"When the humans started enslaving the beast men and other races en masse, treating us as lower species, untouched by the 'lord of light' they created the slave collars that had been banned for generations," Etheras said.

"To use slave collars on other races..." Anthony shook his head. "I can do your Eyes of Truth, but it would just be us and one other in the room, and what you see would have to be sworn to secrecy," Anthony said.

Etheras felt like this human was between a rock and a hard place.

"The rest of you leave us. Ralo, lock the door behind them," Etheras said. *This human is interesting. If he tries to escape, Ralo might be skittish but even he can fight against five humans and still win as long as they don't call on their familiars.*

The guards left the room. The one who had dropped the tool on his foot tried to hide the hobble before the door closed and locked behind them.

Anthony stepped out of the rack with a series of snapping noises, breaking the manacles that were holding him, and waved his arm that still had a manacle stuck on it.

Etheras and Ralo pulled out their weapons as they looked at the Death Knight.

The manacle came apart and embedded itself into the wall as Anthony grabbed his helmet and pulled it off.

"Hey, that hurts. I know I won't win any beauty contests but I'm not *that* bad-looking. I had plenty of girls who liked me when I was younger!" Anthony held his helmet under his arm. As the other two backed away, he moved to the table where the Eyes of Truth was and sat down, putting his helmet down.

"Still think you're older than me, Etheras?" Anthony chuckled as Etheras coughed. "Oh come on, if I wanted to, I could have broken out of those handcuffs at any time. Now you're all scared seeing an undead wandering around?" The light orbs in Anthony's eyes rolled around before he sighed.

Ralo and Etheras felt awkward and they didn't know what to do.

Anthony looked into the Eyes of Truth. "My name is Anthony. I do not wish anyone harm, but if I am attacked or I see injustice then I will assist and kill if needed. I abide by the Guardian's code and I am heading to Ilsal."

Etheras saw that everything that Anthony said was truthful.

"Now I have a few questions for you both." Anthony turned his eyes on them.

Etheras's sword blade twitched. Ralo raised his completely and tugged on the door.

The shadows moved, turning into a mask that had a gloating smile.

Ralo let out a yelping noise, falling on his animal instincts.

"Solomon, stop being a dick." Anthony frowned at the demon face that pouted and faded back into the door.

The doors, the windows—all of it is blocked by that familiar. What kind of familiar is it? A named familiar? Those are the kinds that only the legion commanders of the human armies have.

"So, tell me, how did this start? The fighting between the beast kin and the humans?" Anthony sat back in his chair. "Starting from the war."

"Which war?" Etheras asked, trying to buy himself time as he thought of ways to get out.

"*The* war," Anthony said.

"The war when the races were supposed to have united against a common enemy, that folklore?" Ralo said, panicking.

"Yes, that war," Anthony said.

Etheras's heart jumped. *Was he part of that war? Was he on their side? On our side?*

He felt that this Anthony wouldn't kill them and he was interested to see what his reaction would be. Etheras cleared his throat and started to explain quickly.

"The races were peaceful. The elves continued to be secretive; the dwarves went to their mountains. Gnomes wandered the lands and the goblins moved from place to place as hunting patterns dictated. The humans and the beast kin settled down, reclaimed lands, grew in population. Then the humans started to make trade policies and treaties with different beast kin groups, bribing officials and using other means to get the beast kin to unknowingly sell out their own people.

"A trader who had connections to powerful families used those agreements to gain power. He worked with his fellow traders and his countrymen, as well as their *church*, and took over control of the lands to the west, controlling the trades there.

"He stopped hiding his own greed and his desire to turn beast kin and other races into his slaves. The beast kin rallied together and created a border. We didn't know who was part of his group or not, so we evicted them all and gathered our strength. They sent our own people wearing slave collars at us. Those that they captured, they turned into meat shields. We had to kill people from our own clans under the effect of the slave collars. By that time, he had created a proper military and named himself as emperor, advancing his army to the cities along the border, raiding to kidnap our people and sell them in his markets. Killed people in the street; said that they were devil worshippers. Created devil hunters, part of the church to search out and destroy evil, kill beast kin and those who care about them. Even kill people accidentally, because someone blames them for an unfounded crime. Human *justice* for their job, to cleanse and purify the land."

"What did the beast kin do?" Anthony asked, the flames that rested where his eyes had been flickered from time to time, but without facial expressions it was hard to figure out what he was thinking.

"We called the clans once again. We created a border and made sure our people were safe. The human emperor and his Church of Light are an infection, one that can only be cut out. The cost would be too high, so we build our strength and wait."

Anthony shook his head and pulled his helmet back on. "It seems that Guardians are in great demand. Once I've finished in Ilsal, I'll have to return to have a talk with this human emperor." Anthony stood and raised his hand.

There was a whistling noise and then a crunch as the blade came through a wall.

"Whoops, sorry about the wall." Anthony shook the scabbard, clearing it of dust. He affixed it to his belt.

"Okay, so to protect my identity and current predicament, I'll need the two of you to swear an oath where you promise not to tell anyone about me being all bony and stuff. Also that you won't let anyone know what you've told me. To everyone else, this was just a routine questioning. Do you have any more questions you want me to clarify?" Anthony asked.

Etheras felt as though nothing were under his control ever since the other guards had left. "Do you intend to harm us or our families or people we care about?" Etheras asked.

Anthony pulled off his helmet and looked into the Eyes of Truth. "I promise that I do not intend either of you harm, or your families." Once again, his words rang true.

Etheras relaxed a bit more. *He answered all of our questions and although he had some of his own, he really doesn't intend us harm. No one can lie when looking into the Eyes of Truth device. He hasn't used any spells or any secret arts.*

Etheras put his sword away.

"Captain?" Ralo said in a high-pitched voice.

"Put the blade away and swear the oath," Etheras said. "If he wanted to, he could have killed us long ago."

"Not that I want to!" Anthony waved his finger at them. "Why is it because you're strong, people always think you want to go and destroy everything! I was perfectly happy being a gardener, but no! I had to go and be a Guardian! Well, it was to impress a girl, but that's not the point!"

Seeing Anthony flustered, Etheras's last apprehension fell away.

"I will not reveal the contents of our chat here, your abilities, or the fact that you're undead as long as you do nothing malicious," Etheras said.

"Fair," Anthony said.

Power congealed around Etheras. A piece of power winked into his body. He felt it enter his soul, binding him.

Etheras looked at Anthony. "What is this?"

"A soul binding oath. I've had plenty of people make an oath and then as soon as I let them go, then they turn on me. Don't worry—if you look at it closely, you'll see that my oath is involved in it as well. Guardian's oath, so pretty much covers everything," Anthony said.

Etheras studied the bond on his soul. He could feel it linking them together, a pact between the two of them.

Etheras looked at Ralo.

Ralo shakily lowered his sword. "I swear the same oath as Captain Etheras."

The power within the room distorted and Etheras could feel a new oath was created.

"Right, now, my next question: have there been any issues in the area? It is my job to keep the peace, help out and all of that," Anthony asked.

"Everything is good. I heard that there was a problem in the city Fissat," Etheras said.

"Hmm, okay. I'll take a look at it. Will I need papers or something?" Anthony asked.

"Uh, yes." Etheras pulled out a few documents, putting down Anthony's name; then he signed off on it before he used his seal on it and passed it to Anthony. He didn't feel tense or threatened by him, even though the beast part of his brain was screaming out in danger.

"Thanks! Hope you have a good day." Anthony tapped the papers to his helmet as he walked to the doors. The shadows were sucked into his armor before he opened the doors.

"'Scuse me, sorry, coming through!" Anthony said, holding up his papers, as the guards moved forward.

"Let him pass !" Etheras growled.

The beast kin moved out of the way, shooting questioning looks at Etheras and the pale Ralo.

"Now what?" Ralo asked.

"Keep your oath, or else you'll die," Etheras said in a low voice.

Ralo shivered and closed his mouth.

***

Aila looked up as Ramona lifted her head and looked in a direction, looking happy as she turned her head to Aila.

Tommie was at a stall, bartering with the sheep beast kin.

"One silver and fourteen coppers, best I can do," the sheep kin said.

"Ah, fine deal!" Tommie reached into his bag and pulled out the money.

The sheep kin took it and quickly gave Tommie a bottle of brown sludge. "Good doing business with you," the sheep kin said.

"Have a good day!" Tommie stored the sludge away.

"Ramona's all perked up. Looks like she wants to go somewhere," Aila said.

"I didn't hear any fighting," Tommie said.

"Probably best we go and check out whatever has her all interested."

"Okay." Tommie held out a snack for his mount, who wolfed it down happily.

Tommie got on his back, patting him. "Who's a good boy," Tommie said.

The lizard cub let out a pleased cry and shook his shoulders, happy with the praise.

Aila's mount looked at her with a pouting expression.

"Uh, I don't have any treats." Aila opened her hands with an airy laugh and weak smile.

She only seemed to pout more as she hung her head.

Aila could basically read her thoughts: *Why didn't I get a rider who had more treats? What's the use of this one?*

Ramona let out a croak and started walking down a street; her children followed, with Aila and Tommie along for the ride.

They rode down the street, headed out of Enni.

Anthony walked out of the alleyway and grabbed Ramona's harness, mounting her.

"Well, should be three days' ride to the coast and we can get a boat from there," Anthony said, as if he had been in the saddle the entire time.

"Huh? What—how? When did they let you go? Why?" Aila asked.

"Just a quick chat. Got me some papers, too. Certified nice human!"

"So, you're free to go, just like that?" Tommie asked.

"It took some convincing, but they were okay with it," Anthony said.

"Good thing I got that deal. Where we going to next? I heard that they have the ore that I need in Ilsal, only place outside of the dwarven mountains, and they hold onto it like, like, uhh... well..."

"Like dwarves?" Anthony answered.

"Well, yeah." Tommie shrugged.

"Building materials are finite. They don't like to let anything go in case it might go to waste. Biggest hoarders I ever did know. Good people, but they treat their storage rooms with the same respect they have for their ancestors," Anthony said.

"I've only run into them at the under-market," Aila said. "Only race I know that don't like the appearance of elves."

"The rougher, more hardcore the dwarf, the better," Anthony said, chuckling to himself. "Straightforward, too."

Ramona led them down a road out of the city.

"Can't we stay for another hour?" Tommie asked.

"Probably not the best idea with me around, people don't really trust human looking knights. Even if I have papers saying I'm a good guy. We can get the items you're looking for in Ilsal, at better prices, too. And your items will sell for a higher price there. Not many people going to be interested by items that were made in Radal right now, I don't think." Anthony sounded almost sad about it.

"Come on, adventures abound!" Anthony said as he smacked Ramona, standing up in her stirrups.

She increased her pace and the two younglings let out excited squeals. The people of Enni watched the trio ride through the streets and head out of the city walls.

***

Captain Etheras stood at the top of the watchtower, watching them heading deeper into Selenus, his expression complicated.

"Keep our oath, Anthony," Etheras said. "Or I'll hunt you down and make sure you remain dead."

Chapter: Changing Times

"Leader Su!" A scout came back, waving at the ram beast kin riding the large bedar beasts that was able to support their weight.

The beasts looked like a mix between beaver, ox, and horse: The head and build of an ox, with longer legs like a horse, but much wider to support the extra weight. The fur, webbed feet, and tail of a beaver allowed them to move through the water as well as on land. They were the mainstay beasts of Selenus, from the warfighting bedar legions to the trading routes across the land.

The scout's bedar was older and looked annoyed at being ridden so hard.

Su's bedar, Phila, let out a grunt in greeting. The other bedar's grunt sounded as if it were filled with complaints.

Su frowned to hold back the smile that threatened to break his grounded exterior and patted Phila. He had come to know these beasts after his time in the legions. He had been wounded and transferred back to the rear to the supply trains, where he learned how to become a trader. He left the legion and worked with one of the traders he knew from his military days before he was able to set up his own trade convoy and do his own routes.

"Calm down there. What was your name again?"

"Dadri, Leader Su," the scout said, his tongue hanging to the side of his dog-like features.

"Were you able to find a place for us to rest tonight?"

"Yes, Leader Su! There is a clearing just off the path with a stream running nearby and it is on a rise so the rain should, uhh, run off?" Dadri said, not sure of the word he was looking for.

"Good. Show Gus the location," Su said.

"Sir!" Dadri rode back to find Gus, another guard.

Dadri was new. Their previous scout had gotten into a fight and had been arrested. Needing to leave, they'd had to hire on a new scout. Dadri was young but he had decent skills.

Seems we've been plagued with accidents: one of our scouts gets arrested, then we break a wagon wheel making us waste a half day repairing it. Thankfully we're not too far behind schedule. Maybe I'm just a paranoid old goat. Su thought to himself.

Gus rode out with Dadri, Gus was a large elephant kin.

He was a strong Elephant kin who'd served with Gus, the two of them working together after their service, creating the core of their trading convoy.

Su reached up to his broken horn, one of the more visible reminders of the wounds that had stopped him from continuing within the warfighting legions.

"Well, you only ache when there's something bad about to happen or it's going to rain. By the clouds, I'll say it's rain." Leader Su nudged Phila, who started walking again.

"Leader Su, have we found a camp yet?" Old Dame Carrie, one of his oldest companions and badger kin, asked as she chewed on some nuts, spitting the shells to the side.

"Dadri, the new lad, found a clearing—sent Gus to check it with him," Su said. Phila greeted the two bedar that were hauling Carrie's wagon.

"How far we behind, you reckon?" she asked, offering him a nut.

He declined as she tossed it back, cracking the shell with her teeth.

"I'd say a half day. We can probably make it up with a few hard days of riding, be an early start next couple of mornings," Su said, shifting in his saddle to get comfortable.

"Ah, it's always late nights and early mornings—best way to stay young!" Carrie laughed.

They rode on in companionable silence. People talked to one another or slept, as the wagons rolled over the well-worn road.

Gus returned sometime later with Dadri.

"Place looks good. The new guy did well," Gus said.

"How far?"

"About an hour. Get there a half hour before dusk at our current pace. We'll need to speed up a bit if we want to set up camp in the day-light," Gus said.

"No camp. We'll ring the carriages tonight," Su said.

"Early start tomorrow then?"

"You reading my mind now?"

"Just known you too long," Gus said, his trunk lifting up as he flapped his ears.

"Making me feel old now!"

"Don't worry, you only look as old as you feel!" Gus headed back to his position in the caravan.

"You!" Su threw some fallen nut shells at the elephant kin, who kept going as if he didn't hear anything.

"Boys will be boys," Carrie said, her fur creasing into laughter lines.

Su smiled but didn't say anything.

"Well, best tell the rest of the convoy," Su said with a harrumph, he clicked his tongue, getting his Bedar to complain as he went back down the convoy to tell the other traders.

***

Su rode ahead with Gus and Dadri as they got closer to the camp area.

He checked the ground before the carriages arrived.

"All right, swing around in here. We'll keep the bedar loose but ready to be hooked up, so make sure that they have spacing to do their business and eat," Su said.

The traders were old hands at this and they followed his instructions, creating a circle of carriages that could act as their temporary camp and their defenses if there were any hungry beasts looking for an easy meal in the night.

There were a number of children with the caravans. The merchants travelled far and some brought their families, unable to bear the time apart. With that, they took on easier routes that were still profitable but safer, with short distances between cities and areas where there were few reports of bandits and aggressive beasts in the area.

The caravans formed a circle as Gus rode in toward Su.

"Any issues?"

"No, but I could hear some people talking back some way and they were heading this way. Don't seem like bandits, just a loud group of friends."

"No need for us to do anything then. This area is pretty safe," Su said as he got off Phila.

Gus joined him as they started releasing the straps on their bedars.

"I'll get a list up for the watch and check on the perimeter, not like you won't in another hour."

Su didn't say anything, focusing on brushing down Phila and getting some of the dust out of her fur.

Everyone gathered together as they created fire pits and started to gather firewood and prepare the night's meals.

When in the cities, we fight one another for every copper, but out here we're just people travelling from one place to another.

Su saw Dadri moving from group to group, introducing himself and meeting with different people in the group.

Su sat back, relaxing against his bedroll and the side of the carriage when he heard someone walk up toward him. "How's it going, Carrie? Have you got dinner yet?" he asked, hearing the familiar steps of his friend.

"Thought that I might as well get both of our servings, with how bad you are at forgetting when to get food." She passed him two bowls of stew with hard bread stuck in them, softening. She groaned and sighed as she lowered herself to the ground, leaning against the carriage.

The bedar looked up from their eating to see whether there were any treats before they went back to eating their prepared food again.

"Another week, another city," Su said.

"The life of a trader," Carrie said.

They both started to eat as they got comfortable and ready for bed, knowing that it wouldn't be long until they had to wake up again.

Su looked up as someone stumbled across the camp.

"Looks like someone had a bit more to drink with their food," Carrie said in a knowing tone.

Su pulled out a pipe and started to prepare it and pack it. He heard someone fall. He looked over to see a guard who had been sitting on a carriage had fallen off.

Su put his pipe away, frowning. "It's one thing for the merchants, but the guards..." he said as he got to his feet.

Carrie left him to it as he walked over toward the man. He got a few steps before his head started to spin.

"What?" His vision was swimming. He reached out, trying to stabilize himself, but his legs only collapsed beneath him and he was on all fours, looking around.

"How did I get here? Wasn't I standing?" Su turned back to look at the badger. "Carrie?" Her eyes were closing slowly and then flashing open.

"Poison," Gus said as he wandered into the camp, stumbling.

"Poi—" Reality hit Su, clearing his mind for a few moments. It wasn't long enough for him to completely collect his thoughts. One second, he was trying to move forward; the next, he was opening his eyes to a very different scene.

His head was still blurry, trying to pull information from the sights and the sounds around him and draw upon the half-faded memories, his mouth working before his mind fully processed.

"Poison...watch out...Gus...go warn the...where...what's happening?" Su looked around. Everyone was in some kind of underground area. There was writing on the floor. Fires around the room showed they were broken into different groups: the guards and stronger merchants, the women, the children, the remaining smaller merchants and guards.

Then there were the rough-looking people wearing worn cloaks, who were around the outside of the people, penning them in like beasts.

Su moved around, slowly becoming fully conscious. He, like all of the others, had been hog-tied with a strong rope, making it impossible to escape.

There were people moving around the cavern, all of them were wearing the same color cloaks, all of them were from the same group.

"You did well," a powerful-looking human said, patting Dadri's back. There was no longer the innocence of youth in the new scout's eyes.

Instead, there was a dark and sadistic look that covered his expression as he looked over the merchants.

The women averted their eyes and the children cried out in fear.

The other robed followers smiled and laughed, enjoying what was just a game to them.

"Thank you, master." Dadri bowed his head to the man.

Cultists? Su thought, a thread of fear filling his stomach as he looked at the people around him, scared for those with him.

He looked at the floor, the altars, the runes that were carved into the ground, they weren't raiders, and it looked like some kind of ritual. Which made him think of cultists.

The man sent Dadri among the ranks of the cultists and stepped forward so all of the traders could see him.

"Don't worry, your lives will serve a greater cause. Instead of pining for wealth and riches, you will create chaos, create a new Dena for us all. All things come from chaos and all things will return to it. This is our fate! This is our destiny!" The man raised his hands up and lights of different colors appeared from his body, as though he was filled with a million glowing lights trying to burst free.

The lead cultist stifled a cough. Blood appeared on his teeth as he smiled.

Su shot a look over at Gus, whose eyes moved to Su's broken horn and his bindings.

It was hard to move hog-tied, but he could roll over and flop about like a fish.

Su looked to the others, capturing their eyes; he'd need them to make a ruckus.

One let out a yell and jumped forward; the others joined in as Su and Gus used the cover, getting close to each other. Su braced his head against the floor, making it look as if he were stuck as Gus contorted his body bit by bit, cutting his bonds.

"Silence!" The "master" waved his hand.

The cultists stepped out and kicked or punched the restrained guards on the ground, sending dirt into their eyes and noses. With their limited ability to breathe, they started coughing and panicking.

"Cultists! Power of chaos! Nothing but bandits, child killers, and murderers!" Carrie had somehow got rid of the rope that was meant for her mouth.

"You *dare* to call us bandits! We are leading Dena into a new future. We're more paladins than those puppets of the Light!"

Carrie started laughing, forcing it out.

Su caught her eye. All the attention was on her, allowing Gus to work harder. The rope was nearly broken.

"Puppets? You're the real puppets! Nothing but a bunch of idiots, believing in one another's lies so that you can rationalize killing others for some greater good. You don't have a cause—you have an *excuse*!"

The master raised his hand; a brilliant ray of color shot out and hit Carrie.

She screamed out as her body started to contort and change. Her bones broke and her fur burned away.

Gus and Su screamed against their bindings as those near Carrie leapt back in fear.

The master coughed; it was wetter now. He looked tired, but his eyes were still filled with that crazed look as he stepped forward toward Carrie's broken body.

"That's better. Don't worry, your ignorance has been cleansed with the power of chaos." His eyes fell on everyone lying down. "You'll *all* be saved by the power of chaos, and I must thank you for your selfless sacrifices!"

The traders all tried to move, to escape as the cultists moved among them once again, kicking them back.

Gus worked harder to break his bonds, his and Su's eyes resolute.

Even if we die, I'll take at least one of these bastards down!

***

Anthony's head snapped to the side, staring through the trees as if they didn't exist.

"What is it?" Aila asked.

"Cultists of the chaos lords." Anthony's voice was perfectly cold as he wrapped his hand around his sword.

"What?" Tommie asked.

"Stay here. I'll handle this."

"Aren't we supposed to work together? You make too much noise in that armor. I can scout it out," Aila said.

"I can watch the gear!" Tommie's voice was shaking, his face pale.

Anthony could tell he was terrified of possibly getting into a fight. *Not everyone is a warrior.*

"Thank you, Tommie, Aila. I will take you up on both of those offers. Solomon can help you with getting closer to the cultists. They should have a warren or something that they're using to stay hidden.

With the power that they're using, they must be up to something and by the markings back a ways on the road, there was a caravan moving down this way not long ago," Anthony said, looking at Aila. His glowing eyes froze her. "Time is of the essence, Aila Wranoris."

Aila quickly got down as the shadows moved. In the darkness, she could barely make out Solomon as he wrapped around her. She could *feel* him, darkness mana, wrapping around her like a wet towel.

"Wow, I can hardly see you unless I'm looking right at you. You blend into the night perfectly." Tommie said.

"It should be much easier for you to hide. The more Solomon shakes, the easier it will be for you to be seen. He can guide you to the location of the cultists. If you need me, just tell Solomon and he has his way of getting a message to me," Anthony said.

"I'll be back soon." Aila stepped forward and ducked into the underbrush. She moved through the forest. Her light footsteps were soundless as she flitted across the ground like a specter.

She passed a cleared area. There were carriages all in a circle, with bedars tied up and sleeping. Fires smoked half drowned out with water to stop their light from being seen by others.

She moved to the nearby stream, her eyes glowing as she used a tracking spell. "There you are." She found an entrance hidden behind a boulder, leading downward.

Her feet stopped as she discovered a magical trap at the entrance. "Crude and elementary." She checked around as she started to disable the trap.

Aila heard screams as she disabled the simple trap formation and stepped into the cave system. She moved through the tunnels, following the noises and then the person speaking. "Solomon, get ready."

The darkness moved around her.

She snuck forward, taking time to listen to make sure that there was no one around the corners before she moved. In her right hand, she held her curved dagger; in her left, she had prepared a spell but hadn't activated it so there was no light being given off.

"Solomon, tell Anthony," she said as she saw the cultists kicking the people into order as one man walked up to a pedestal in the middle of the room.

Solomon disappeared in a second. There was no wind but his speed was like an arrow being released from a bow.

Aila studied the formation that held the people inside and the items that were on the pedestal to be used to activate it. *This is some kind of magical manipulation and there are elements of death magic mixed in.* She shuddered, looking at the people.

I need to do something before they're able to use the formation. Bow—can maybe get off a few shots before they start fighting back. I can raise a few golem shells and then give them souls to increase their fighting abilities. The spell takes a lot more mana. I'll have to take the risk of being found out. Anthony must be on his way.

There were people in tattered robes around the outside of the formation and those who were moving between the sections of the formation.

She took out items from her pouch that would accelerate her spell and increase the strength of the created creatures.

***

Su and Gus watched the master stepping up to the stage; he was preparing himself. Gus had been able to cut through one binding and was working on another, looking for an opportunity.

The master raised his arms as Gus's tribal tattoos flared to life, giving him immense strength; he broke through his bonds and tore apart Su's bindings. He charged forward as the cultists yelled in alarm, some pulling out their blades.

The master looked back as Gus crossed the formation.

"Come on." Su had activated his tribal tattoos. Old power flooded into him as he increased in size. He used his hands and his horn to cut the bindings, freeing another who rushed forward as well, their tattoos flaring to life.

"Halt," the master said as the formations activated.

Su's hands were frozen, picking up another guard, as Gus's charge was halted, frozen in mid-stride.

"Why must you fight your destiny!" the master yelled out. His body glowed with those multiple colors and his power seemed to be fluctuating wildly.

"Dadri!" The master waved forward the young beast kin.

He bowed to the master and pulled out a small blade; he walked freely into the formation and stood before Gus, turning his head to the side. "Don't worry, I'll take my time," he said.

"Let him go or I'll kill your man!" A female voice came from the other side of the room.

The cultists all looked over to see a woman in the shadows, holding a cultist. Her dagger shone against the flickering light of the underground ritual room.

"Chaos lives!" the master yelled, signaling to Dadri.

A cold look appeared in his eyes as he looked at the woman, locking eyes with her. He reached out with his dagger and slowly inserted it into Gus's stomach; he cried out against the magical binding of the formation.

There was a flash of light between the chaos cultists and the woman.

Three gray spell formations rotated on the ground, making everyone look at them. Stones rose up from the ground, forming together into humanoid creatures.

"Destroy the golems and kill her!" the master said in a cold voice.

The cultists ran forward. Dadri joined them and left Gus, while the cultist in the woman's grip twisted in her arms.

She drew her dagger across his neck and he dropped to the ground, screaming. Her hand was wrapped in purple, drawing out his soul and turning it into a tool. She closed her fist, destroying the consciousness within and turning it into fuel for her own spell.

Three threads of purple shot out from her hand and struck the golems.

Purple lines burned into their surface and filled their eyes as they reached down, grabbing stone spears from the ground.

The woman moved back. A golem stood in the way of the cultists. It threw a spear, the stone spear pierced a dagger wielding cultist and had the force to pin another to the wall.

It reached down with its opposite hand the ground rose under its hand forming a spear for it to grasp.

The cultists continued to charge, drawing upon familiars or their bloodlines to empower their bodies.

The golems spear took out another cultist its hands sharpening into blades as it met the cultists that closed with it.

The master started chanting and returned to his position on the altar. The different reactants were consumed by the formation to power the ritual functions.

Su watched as power started to drain from the formation sections containing the women, children, and traders, routing back to the altar.

The people there started to look fatigued and tired, their very life force being dragged away. That pure energy was twisted with the power of the altar and routed toward the section with the guards.

That multicolored light of chaos started to reach out from the ground, entering their bodies.

They let out yells as they started to change and grow. A new twisted power entered their bodies, eroding their minds.

Two of the golems advanced toward the altar. Although they were smarter than other golems he had seen, they were still big and not agile. The cultists were being killed, but there had to be nearly fifty of them.

They worked the golems, chipping away at their blind spots and weakening them. Even if a few of their numbers were killed, it clearly didn't matter to them.

She was being pushed back. Her main golem was fighting the good fight, but he was being worn down faster than the others. He'd lost one arm already and his side was being torn into.

The woman was fast and deadly, mixing in spells with her close-in fighting style. Two had already been claimed by her blade.

A roar shook the entire ritual room. A light, like a sun, appeared through one of the tunnels.

A dragon appeared and shot out of the tunnel. A man shot out from its body; he reached out and the dragon turned into a ray of light as it wrapped around the man's armor.

He drew his sword as the shadows distorted around him, his right side armor covered in brilliant golden flames, while shadows writhed around on his left leg, their light visible through his armor.

When he looked up, his right eye glowed black, while the left was golden. Black and Golden mana wrapped together around his body.

The master looked over at the knight. "Don't let them interrupt the ritual!" He went back to chanting, speeding it up.

The human knight rushed forward. He turned into a ghostly specter of shadow, flashing past the cultists. His blade extended out; the cultist, unable to stop their momentum, struck the blade.

The man tore the blade out of their chest; he deflected one blade, kicking a man's shin. His blade lashed out, cutting their neck. They dropped to the ground as he spun, striking a man in the face with his elbow and kicking another in the side.

His blade stabbed out, piercing the second in the neck as his knee crumbled. He reversed his blade with such speed that it sung in the air; he slammed it under his arm and it pierced through their robe and the cultist's chest.

He seemed to evaporate and reappear with an arrow in his hand. He turned and threw it back at the archer. It was covered in golden flames, a streak of light as it struck the archer.

Su looked back and two more were lying on the ground, dead.

The other cultists looked over at the fighting, giving the woman the opening she needed.

She dropped low. Her dagger shot out, piercing underneath a man's armpit; she grabbed his other shoulder, turning his back as he turned forward into the new wound in his shoulder.

Her blade went through the opposite side of his neck and came out with a spray of blood. She kicked him into another attacker near her golem.

The attacker stumbled into the golem's range as it kicked the cultist, breaking his body. It threw a spear, passing the woman by inches; she shot out a water spell, catching a cultist in the face. The water formed around their face and they clawed at it, trying to pull it off.

The other golems didn't try to advance anymore, instead using their bodies to draw and hold in as many cultists as possible so they couldn't stop the ranger woman and the knight.

Dadri appeared in front of the man. He let out a breath on the powder in his hand, a powerful poison that covered the man's body.

Dadri had a gloating smile on his face as the man shot forward a flickering shadow that resolved into a man right before Dadri, before he had time to react a golden light pierced Dadri's throat and came out of his spine.

His gloating smile turned into one of confusion.

Su took a violent appreciation to seeing the man's world turned around, seeing him the victim instead of the attacker. He didn't know how to deal with it.

The man's blade slid out as he ran forward, turning into a blur of flames and shadows before slamming into a barrier around the altar.

"You'll never be able to break through in time." The master sneered as the last of the materials on the altar were being consumed.

Su would have bent over in pain if he could move. Instead, he cried out in his head and between his teeth, feeling that foreign and alien power invading his body, changing him.

The knight lashed out, threads of black and gold around his sword as he slammed it against the barrier, throwing up a gale that made it hard for any of the cultists to get close to him.

"Bruce! Give me your strength!" the man yelled out.

An earthly power that resonated with Su seemed to awaken within the man. It stilled one's fear and gripped their stomach, causing one to feel the blood rushing through their veins, the vitality and power held within their bodies.

A silhouette of an ox appeared behind the knight as the green section of the tree on his back seemed to turn into real tree bark instead of just an elegant carving.

Threads of deep-green power spread through the knight's legs and joined the power on his sword. A green tracing of an ox was drawn out on his left arm. Its eyes opened and turned to face the master.

The knight drew in power from the room and struck out: one man's and three familiars' power concentrated and working together.

The power rippled through the mana barrier and cut into it. It shattered in a line like glass, ripples of destruction radiating off the strike.

"You!" The master's body fluctuated wildly as chaotic power rippled through his body. Unable to contain it in his emotional state, he grew rapidly, reaching nine foot in height. His eyes blazed with chaotic power as tears across his body leaked out power.

The knight was thrown back by the force of the shield breaking.

He dug his feet into the ground as he slammed into several cultists.

The golden light and the black shadows evaporated outside of his body, turning into the dragon and a devil-like mask.

The mask and the Dragon worked together the mask appeared in their blind spots, shadows from behind the mask turning into blades that would send attacks at its opponent's blind spots.

The dragon let out a roar, and breathed out fire, its claws cut down any of those that too close.

"You good, Aila?"

"Yeah!" the woman yelled back.

The knight turned and yelled as he threw his sword like a lightning bolt. The sword was covered in green energy as a ox silhouette appeared around it, its horns in line with the blade. It sunk into the altar. The convergence of power sent green energy through the cracking altar, causing it to explode and rain down.

The energy that had been invading Su was released, rushing back to the altar and then back to the others. Their appearances started to re-cover but they dropped to the ground, drained and unable to move.

Su dropped to the ground, feeling drained.

"For the clans!" Gus said weakly as he tried to force himself to stand.

The others stood, their tattoos blazing with power as they let out a yell.

"Half of you, protect the others!" Su yelled as he checked on Gus.

"Go!" Gus said, pushing him aside angrily.

Su nodded and ran forward, grabbing a hammer from a cultist's body.

Su felt his old power coming back. His instincts to fight increased as the weakness in his body was left behind. He was a warrior of the clans!

They rushed forward. The cultists had pale faces, seeing everything come apart around them. They weren't trained fighters; if they were, they wouldn't have needed to resort to poisons and sleeping powders.

The beast kin ran together. Their bodies blazed with power as their tattoos enhanced their abilities and drew out their bloodlines.

The ground shook as Su let out a war cry and lowered his head. He smashed a spear to the side with his hammer and hit the cultist's shield, sending them flying on their back. He struck out with his hammer, cracking another's skull, their body being tossed to the side.

Su got a cut on the shoulder as he failed to dodge a blade. The cultist beast kin swung their blade back, aiming to cut Su's ribs.

Another guard hacked at the cultist's neck and cut him down.

The guards were cut and wounded, but they fought on, relying on their tattoos to gain the power they needed to keep on fighting.

The majority of the cultists were human. Their familiars were twisted and corrupted; their attacks were confused and erratic, allowing them to get in hits.

The knight had charged forward and met with the chaos-altered master.

The devil mask and the dragon raced through the cultists, landing hits and helping out as they could.

The man unleashed a powerful attack with his fist, the air distorting around him.

The Knight reached out his hand, a hum filled the air, the Knight's blade hit his hand the momentum taking him out of the master's path of attack as he cut out with his sword, driving it into the man's stomach.

The master let out a surprised scream.

The knight pulled out his sword. He dropped down and forward; his blade cut clean through the master's leg.

The Master landed on the floor and rolled to the side, sending blasts of chaotic power at the knight.

The pain made his actions wild and panicked.

The Knight's sword intercepted the attacks, deflecting them with practised ease, they were unequally matched.

Blasts struck the ground, leaving smoking craters as the Knight advanced and the glow of the master started to decline, his body was starting to show signs of falling apart, his power decreasing.

The master raised both of his fists and a spell formation appeared.

The knight shot forward and pierced that formation with his sword. A golden light consumed the power of the spell.

His sword flashed, smacking the man's arms into the ground. The ground came up, moving like a snake, wrapping around the master and his body, drawing him into the ground slightly.

Su looked up from his fighting. He had blood in his eye and there were bruises and cuts all over his body, but as long as he didn't get an infection, he should be fine.

Two guards had died in the fighting, but no more cultists remained.

The light dimmed around the knight. As it did, one could see a faint purple symbol of an eye on a shield on his chest.

"Y-you—how? You all died!"

"Ah, you don't know the half of it," the knight said with a cold laugh. "It's good to be remembered, though—seems that not all of the memories of us have faded."

"Guardian, you might have come back from the dead but the chaos has been here this entire time!" the master spat back.

"Then I have a lot of work to do. I had a fear I would get bored." The knight reached out and put his hand on the master's head. Golden flames spread through the man's body, consuming his chaotic power and destroying him from the inside.

The knight turned toward where the altar was and reached out his hand. A spell formation appeared there. As he moved his hand, its complexity increased and the formation changed. The formation used for the ritual drew in power from the cultists' bodies, turning them into dust that disappeared with the slightest wind.

Their energy congealed into the formation that glowed green and blue.

Su couldn't help but feel relaxed seeing it, even with the immense power that was building up.

The knight placed his hand on the formation. A powerful life force energy spread out. Motes of light floated away from the knight, like seeds of a flower being released upon a strong summer breeze.

Su felt it entering his body. His wounds healed at a visible rate; the aches, the fatigue of his body recovered. The strength and life force he had lost was returned and increased; even his horn started to regrow.

He looked around and saw the rest of the traders recovering. The dead didn't rise, but the wounded recovered quickly.

Su turned and rushed over to Gus, who was looking at his side, wiping away the blood to show his side had recovered completely.

Su dropped to his knees and examined him.

He didn't know what to do; relief rushed through his body.

They didn't need to say anything as Gus held out a hand. Su took it; the two of them embraced and slapped each other's backs.

The golem's purple light went out as they collapsed into piles of rocks.

The woman's clothes were showed blood stains and where daggers had been able to get past her defenses, but she stood up straight, her minor wounds recovered.

"Who is your leader?" the knight asked.

"I am," Su said, standing straighter.

"I suggest that we make sure that everyone has recovered, get some food into them and then we leave at first light. My companions and I are heading to Skalafell and to the northeast," the knight said.

"We're intending to go to Skalafell as well," Su said. His eyes caught Carrie's body.

The knight saw her body and walked over to her. He placed his hands on her. Magic power entered her body; her body became whole again, a peaceful look on her face.

"Thank you," Su said, choking on his words.

"Everyone deserves to be treated with respect," the knight said. "See to your people." The man cocked his head to the side. "We found your carriages."

"My name is Su. What is your name?"

"I'm Anthony, and this is Aila. Our other companion is Tommie," Anthony said.

"Thank you for saving our lives." Su tilted his head to them both, a sign of great respect, placing his life in their hands with complete trust.

"It is my duty. All people of Dena fall under my protection." Anthony sheathed his sword. "I'll check on those carriages and make sure that none of the cultists escape. There might have been some of them scouting."

Su nodded as Anthony and Aila walked together down a tunnel. He didn't miss how the shadows moved oddly around them and several shadows seemed to shoot out of the tunnel ahead of them.

Thinking of the familiar shadow the knight wielded Su felt a shiver run through him.

"Saved by a human—who would have thought," Gus said, next to Su.

Su grunted, but his eyes followed their shadows before they turned a corner, disappearing from sight.

His eyes turned to his people. People were crying and holding one another. The guards were fanned out, watching the entrances. Everyone was still tense, a chaotic mix of emotions.

"See to Carrie. Once Anthony and Aila return, we'll move to the carriages," Su said.

Gus gave off a low whistle of acknowledgement and headed to carry out his tasks.

Chapter: Memories

Su postponed leaving the next day. They spent the night gathering wood, building pyres for those who had passed away.

There were no long speeches; instead, several people closest to those who had passed away held torches.

Su stood in the front, next to Carrie's pyre.

"To the lost," Su said, as everyone else responded: "But never forgotten."

The torches were lowered, catching on the wood.

The flames quickly grew. Waves of heat came off the pyres and smoke rose into the dawn sky.

Some cried in the crowd; others watched with stony expressions as they saw those pyres burning on the side of the stream.

Aila turned to Anthony. "Those cultists—they said that they were Agents of Chaos."

Anthony let out a tired sigh at her unasked question. "They're nothing more than the minions for the true Agents of Chaos. Their sole purpose is to create infighting among the people of Dena to weaken us before their gates can bridge the gap between our worlds again."

"Who are they, though, and how do they know you?"

"They're a race from another place that invade our lands, looking to consume the power of Dena. They consumed all of the power of their own home, so they want to destroy ours. They know me because the Guardians were originally just a ragtag group of warriors who upheld a certain code, but with the unification of Dena, we were drafted in to be Guardians, creating an oath and swearing to uphold it to create stability for the people of Dena.

"Our duty was to fight the chaos destroying our backlines, so that the front could remain strong and united. Though based on the master's memories, it looks like there were some who were left here, or they had a few hidden gates that they sent a few Agents of Chaos over in. They've been building strength. They're one cell, or group of people, that are part of a vast and complicated network that looks to hide among the population, gaining positions of influence to carry out acts to create instability between people.

"The Agent of Chaos told them about Guardians, and he also said how they were able to destroy us and remove us even from history so that we will never be reformed..." Anthony's words trailed off.

"Something wrong?"

"Oh, there are a lot of things that are wrong. I feel like there is a memory I have that's linked to it, but I just can't seem to bring it into focus. How frustrating."

"You've made a lot of progress already in recovering your memories, but how were you able to read the master's?" Aila asked.

"Just an ability I have—keep the person off-balance and I can draw out a lot of their memories. The surface ones, the ones they're thinking of right at that moment, are the strongest. It was why I showed my emblem, see if there was anything triggered. Thankfully I was able to get some useful bits."

Aila looked to Tommie, who was looking at his feet. "Are you okay?" Aila asked.

"Am I okay? I was too scared to act. I just stayed with Ramona and her children, looked after them. I was scared stiff, didn't know what to do, wanted to run or hide. Every noise made me flinch." Tommie sunk lower.

"It's okay to be scared and afraid. You could've run, but you stayed there and watched over Ramona and her children. I was terrified, thinking that I could die, but I just did as I was trained to and kept on fighting," Aila said.

"But you were trained to fight. You're an elf—best fighters in the woods—and he's a knight with familiars and powers." Tommie built up before deflating. "And I'm just a gnome. I wanted to build the Gnome-inator, thinking that it would give me the confidence I needed to become like you two, to become a hero or a champion. Instead, when a challenge arose, I hid instead of doing anything."

"Why did you follow us?" Anthony asked.

"To challenge myself," Tommie said.

"The real reason. You had a comfortable life, you had a job—why did you give that up to follow two basic strangers?" Anthony asked.

"I..." Tommie's face moved in different ways, as if trying to somehow communicate thoughts, emotions, and ideas into one cohesive collection of words.

People started to head back to the carriages as Anthony and Aila looked at Tommie, waiting.

"I always tell people about the places that I've been and things that I've seen but the truth is that I have only seen a few things and gone to a few places. I want to see and do more. I have few attachments. I was working with the merchants because I wanted to get parts for my Gnome-inator. When I heard that you were going to the capital of the elves, I was interested by the story that I could tell others..

"My dad always says that my mother left us, but I know the truth: she was killed in a troll attack. He wasn't strong enough to stand up for her and I wanted to be strong enough to stand up to others. I see gnomes and the smaller people always being stepped on, so I wanted to build something that would allow us to be respected, that would allow us to stand up to the powerful people in the world. You're both strong, so I hoped that I could tag along, going to different places, getting the parts that I need to build my Gnome-inator. Then I can go home, tell people stories about other places, and sell my Gnome-inator design so that other gnomes and smaller races can defend themselves. I'd be rich and live a comfortable life," Tommie said.

"All right." Anthony nodded.

"All right?" Tommie asked, looking up at them. "But I used you. I saw you as if you were guards, a way for me to go from place to place to build my machine."

"Going on an adventure, leaving the place you're comfortable—it's not easy. It can also be dangerous. You're not a bad person and you've stuck up for us. You don't have any malicious intent and it is okay to be scared. I've been scared plenty of times. I was the weakest person in my village. Looking to build something to help others is a noble cause. Yes, you're looking to make money off it, but you need money to live and you can use that to buy more supplies and continue building. Also, there is a gnome mechatronics academy in Ilsal, I believe—at least, there used to be. It might be a good place for you to get leads on your project," Anthony said.

Tommie looked stunned and looked at Aila.

"Hey, I always welcome someone else along. Helps keep me sane. I'd have lost it if it was just Anthony and me this long." Aila shrugged.

Tommie let out a mix between a cough and a laugh as Anthony's eyes thinned into lines through his helmet.

***

Su and the loved ones of those who had passed away collected their ashes and they started to hook up the bedar to their carriages and headed down the road toward Skalafell.

A dark cloud hung over the caravan as they moved.

The young children, not understanding what had happened and having little concept of death, were running around, playing with Anthony, bugging Aila, and stealing Tommie's gear.

Tommie spent most of the time chasing them. Due to their similar height, he had to work hard to get the pieces back from them.

They would sleep early, with guards patrolling vigilantly. Everyone slept in their clothes and most had weapons with them as they ate different meals, as if someone would poison them again.

Then, with the crack of dawn, they would pack up and move on. The excited spirit that they had left with had disappeared. Every day wore on them, looking at Skalafell as if it were their savior.

***

"We've been pushing hard. If we push harder, then we can arrive early tomorrow morning," Gus said.

"Your people need to rest," Anthony said, coming up beside Su and Gus on Ramona.

"You've all been through a lot. You understand that with one an-other, but you haven't had time to mourn, to think about it and process it. Once you get into the city, there will be so much to do that everyone will just push it down and it will only get worse. The best way to heal a wound is to clean it quickly before it has time to fester. Aila was able to find a nice camp not far away. If we break early for tonight, I can hunt us some meat, have a night to remember those who were lost, have guards on duty. Aila, Tommie, and I will take the night shift. Go have a few drinks, let out the pain. We'll be close enough to Skalafell that no one will try to do anything." Anthony turned and looked at them.

Su wanted to argue. He wanted to get his people into the city, if only to get the worry off his mind, but hearing Anthony, he could feel the pain inside. He still didn't want to face it.

"If we push on, we'll be able to get into Skalafell and rest sooner," Su said, not willing to face that weakness.

"Are you so scared and weak that you can't confront your own pain with the people who suffered with you?" Anthony asked derisively.

"You!" Su said as Gus's hand reached for his sword dangerously.

"And there—what were you going to do? Cut down the person who saved you over some words? How short is your fuse?" Anthony's voice changed, sounding disappointed as Ramona moved faster.

Su choked on his words, wanting to yell out and punch Anthony to make him take back his words. But he knew violence wouldn't make him take back his words; it would only prove that Anthony's words were right.

It drove all of the fight go out of him. He felt defeated; he felt empty and hollow. He was so tired from driving hard the last few days, he had drained himself so that he didn't have to deal with the emotions that lay below the surface, threatening to make him crumble.

"Check the place and report back to me," Su said, making a decision.

"You sure?" Gus asked.

"He's right. And if they wanted to do anything, he's powerful enough to have done it already," Su said.

"Yeah." Gus sighed. It was clear that he was tired from having his guard up all of the time. They were stretched thin.

***

"Are you sure that this is the best idea?" Aila asked as they turned in to the area that she had scouted out earlier.

"I'm sure it's what they need," Anthony said.

He saw a wall. People stood across it, eyes dull as they looked outside.

Others sat wherever they could, sleeping or eating, dull and numb to reality. There was dried blood on the walls, where others had once stood.

The defenders' armor was scuffed and worn. Many wore bandages but they continued fighting.

Some hid in corners. Their tears fell down, cleaning their dust- and sweat-stained cheeks and cleaning their armor.

The others looked away, not wanting to see them in pain, not wanting to reveal their own pain that was burning them up from inside.

Anthony saw it all as he looked over the wall at the vast plains beyond. There was smoke on the horizon. The chaotic war machine was licking their wounds, gaining their strength, and destroying Dena as they went. There were flashes of multicolored lights in the distance. There were floating islands and other creations in the skies as the clouds rained up and down. The laws that governed Dena were turned and mutated, no longer following the same path that they had for generations, altered by the chaos that now walked upon its surface.

Anthony returned to seeing the carriages as they circled up and the people started to get down, stretching and preparing for the night. They had been riding early until late, so this was one of the few times that they were setting up camp with more than a few hours before it turned dark.

Su got them to build one large campfire and even broke out drinks for the traders. Gus and some of the others were stopped from drinking; they wanted to have people alert, after all.

"If they don't deal with that inner pain, if they push it aside as if it is nothing, then it will tear them apart and they will turn into the Agents of Chaos that the cultists wanted. Lashing out at others in order to try to feel some kind of control over their lives, turning to violence for control."

"How do you know this?" Tommie asked.

"I was like them before," Anthony said.

Tommie went back to tending Ramona and the cubs.

"We're going to have a look around. Yell if there is anything," Anthony said, indicating for Aila to join him.

They walked around the outside of the carriages, looking at the orange-tinted sky as the sun started to go down.

"How do you feel, Aila?" Anthony asked.

"Fine."

"How do you feel about killing those cultists?"

"I—well, I've killed before: bandits, the people in the mountains, others who tried attacking my home."

"And?" Anthony said as the silence dragged.

"Well, they would have hurt me or others I care about. Either I got rid of them or they would have done worse," Aila said.

Anthony nodded. "Fighting for others is easier than fighting for yourself. But how do you feel about it?"

"I don't like doing it, but I've hardened my heart to it. There are plenty of people who die from colds or diseases all of the time. I didn't want to kill them, but I had to," Aila said. "I don't really know how to describe what I feel. It's as if there is a void inside me, but also it's all wound up. I'm scared that something will set me off and I'll fall in a hole. But then, I've gone this far and I haven't had anything happen to me, so I wonder if that fear is unwarranted. But then I feel it, the void and the tension within playing back and forth. Does it change?"

"Not really, you just learn how to balance it better and take the time to blow off steam and talk to others when there are signs of trouble. It's hard for us to know what our issues are. We're always too close to it, but others can help. It's not a weakness but a strength to go to others when you think that there might be something wrong," Anthony assured her.

"Thank you," Aila said in a small voice.

They continued patrolling. They could see through the carriages that people were starting to prepare food; they were talking to one another, small talk, about what they would do when they were in the city, the way that their carriages were riding, what food they were looking forward to, easing the tensions and divisions that had been created over the last few days.

"You're not what I expected," Aila said.

"Hmm?" Anthony looked over to her.

"Well, you know you are a death knight with the heart of a lich inside you, but you're much more than that," Aila said.

Anthony unconsciously put his hand over the heart beating inside his chest. "Thank you." He lowered his hand.

"I never thought that a skeleton could get themselves into so much trouble but also save so many people and help others."

"It doesn't matter who we are—we can all help one another. My actions might have been big but it is the small ones that are the longest lasting," Anthony said.

Aila turned her head to the side. "What do you mean?"

Anthony took some time to respond.

"It is saying hello, it's smiling at others, playing with kids for those few minutes, the time you take to help someone out in everyday life, holding the door. Small, incredibly small things. But if you do them again and again, and if you mean them, then other people will see what you're doing and then, feeling good about it, they will do it when they're greeted by others.

"We become better people when we're looking after one another instead of looking after ourselves.

"This is a part of our communities that we might lose from time to time. The community is not about trying to look good for one another in big acts. It's about the small things for your neighbor, the greeting you give one another. It's not a deep connection, but it is a connection. When you have a bad day and you want to yell at someone, you start to yell, but then you remember that they might be having a bad day, that your taking it out on them might be making them have a bad day. So you take a step back, change your tone and then start again, let them help you instead of being forced to do your bidding. Sympathy is stronger than anger. Aggression can ignite other's anger, but kindness can stick with them in a way that they might not even realize. You can point immediately to the people who made you angry, but it is only at the end of the day that you can reflect on what made you feel better. It isn't a currency; it isn't something that can be bartered or taken away. You have to give it, but unlike money, it will come back to you."

Aila felt that his words were simple but confusing. They also sparked a lot of difficult thoughts as she started to think on her own life, on those times that she had been in the situations he had talked about.

Anthony didn't say anything as they walked around the carriages, as people started to get closer around the fire, starting to pull out their food and cook with one another. They were a broken community, but they were still a community, one that had shared the good and the bad, the hard and the easy times.

Aila looked up at the sky. The faint smoke rose from the fire against the battered carriages and the glowing sky that was a mix of colors. The trees swayed in the breeze. It was cold but refreshing, invigorating her mind.

She felt that something was wrong and she looked at Anthony. She didn't as much *see* something was wrong but she *felt* like it was, that kind of second sense that one would have being around someone else for long enough.

"Is there something wrong?" Aila asked.

Anthony slowed his footsteps. "It's about recovering my memories. I want to have them back, but then, every time I get them back, more times than not, they're filled with disasters, remembering people only to lose them, seeing battlefields, such loss that it hurts. It feels like it's tearing me apart on the inside, but there is also something that is keeping me together." He put his hand on his armor and tapped it. "I don't know what will happen when I recover all my memories."

Anthony joked around and he looked after other people, but it didn't mean that he wasn't affected, that he was numb to everything that was happening. Under the laughter and the humor, there was a man, missing most of his life, trying his best with the memories he had to be the best person he could be. It was no easy task to complete.

"Well, if that time comes, I'll be here to help you," Aila said.

"Thank you." Anthony's voice was just a whisper, but she still heard it as he cleared his nonexistent throat.

"How can you make those noises without a face?"

"Practice, I guess? How can I talk without a tongue or lips? I just have the body—I don't know how it works!"

"How do you not know how it works?" Aila asked as they continued patrolling.

"Well, do you know all of the functions down to the smallest part of your body?"

"Well, that's different!"

They argued with each other, feeling all the better for it, thinking on what they had learned that night.

***

Su looked at the people around the fire. He knew all of them; most of them had travelled together for multiple trips. He had come to know their stories, know their families. As he looked around and saw who wasn't there anymore, his heart twisted.

It was so easy to think that they were just on guard, that they were just away for a few minutes and that they would be back soon. He smiled, thinking of the antics they had gotten up to, the times that they had joked, sleep deprived from one trading fair, or when they had shared a drink after a long day of work. The times he had seen them showing him pictures of their families, told him the stories of how they got to where they were.

Among traders, many had broken lives, had something that they were looking to escape, something that they were going toward. Or they had simply started trading and loved it. Many joined and many stayed, finding that normal life didn't suit them anymore.

Su stood and cleared his throat. Everyone looked over to him, curious what he wanted to keep them here for.

"We all came here for different reasons. Some of you were looking to just get passage to the next city. Some of you have been with me and my group for some time, and we have gone to plenty of cities across Selenus. We lost people a few days ago. We were able to return them to Dena and give them rest. We were able to survive as well, but just as we've completed their rites, it does not mean that we are saved. What

I want to do tonight is to talk—to talk about those we lost, who were they to you, what is weighing on you."

Su looked at them all. There were different looks on their faces, from anger and fear as they remembered the events. Facing one's own mortality was never an easy thing.

"I met Carrie years ago, when she was a trader just setting out in the world. She came to my camp all the time, keeping us supplied. She was working as a supply driver so that she could build up the funds that she needed in order to start her own business.

"She stayed a bit longer and she fell for one of the guys in my cohort. He was like an older uncle to me. His name was Dietrick. We were close, and Carrie and I got along well. When we had time off, we would meet up and wander around, the three of us.

"Dietrick was killed in an attack and Carrie wasn't able to deal with it. She had the money, gave me a way to contact her and she disappeared. I didn't think that I would see her again. When I was injured, they had me working to move supplies. When I was in a city collecting food to be moved up to the front lines, I ran into her again.

"I remember it as if it were yesterday. I was in a dark place, thinking I was useless with my broken body, unable to fight anymore." Su rubbed his leg that no longer throbbed in constant pain.

"She walked right into the supply barn. They wouldn't let her past because she was a civilian, so she yelled my name. 'Su, you useless goat, get your ass out here!' I ran out there, all fired up, only to see her there, tapping her foot on the ground. 'Since you're a merchant, you might as well do it the right way!' she yelled, not letting me get a word in edgewise." Su laughed, even as his eyes were damp. "I thought that I had nothing left. She showed me that there was more in the world to see. I left the military and started to run convoys. She was my first customer. She would never say if she was coming with us to the next place, but every morning before we left, she would be there sitting on her caravan. She was the real boss of the convoy."

Others smiled and laughed, nodding their heads, knowing her antics well as they all lived through their own memories.

"When I first met Tollem, I didn't know if he was really going to sell me a real Ilsal timepiece or if he was having me on. After three rounds of negotiations and me having to put my head back on, he joined the caravan and I got a bunch of healing pills. We left and headed out. I was starting to get annoyed, feeling scammed. When I confronted him, he was scared, not for himself but for me. He insisted that I take the pills. I didn't want to and two days later, I got a case of the shivers. He was there, feeding me the pills and looking after me. He was a trained medic and got busted for selling hooch out of his tent. He had a silver tongue but he was always looking out for people. I had been so confused, I didn't realize that he was trying to help me and had noticed that I had a bad fever and infection. He was one hell of a character, but he was a good person," Gus said.

Slowly, the others—one by one—started telling their stories. They laughed and they cried, not sure what emotions pulled on them as they were unable to control them.

And they didn't have to. Su looked around at them. They had all been through it together. They had dealt with the good times and the bad; they were a dysfunctional, highly erratic, unusual collection of people from all walks of life, but they were family. It didn't matter that they weren't from the same clan, or that their blood wasn't the same: they had created their own tribe and forged their path together.

Su looked up at the sky and saw the stars there. The silver jewels hung above, drawing one away from their mortal body and worries.

He closed his eyes, feeling those who had gone ahead of him, those beyond the veil. It was as if he could see them smiling at him, waiting for him on the other side.

Su raised his glass slightly, poured some on the ground and drank the rest.

He felt as if he had been cleaned from the inside out. The darkness that had crept in had been pushed back. It wasn't totally gone and there was a new scar there, but he felt as if the clouds had parted on a stormy day. With time, the clouds would move away and the sky could clear; he could see that now.

They drank and ate together, breaking down the barriers that had started to form and bringing them back together.

Su excused himself and moved to a quiet corner between carriages. He looked up at the silver stars and the blue moon that hung in the heavens.

He stood like that for some time, organizing his thoughts.

"It doesn't get easier, but I don't think any of us would like it to be easier," Anthony said.

Su didn't know how long he had been there. He didn't turn and continued to look to the stars and moon. "The pain shows just how much we cared for them," Su agreed.

They fell into silence before Su turned to face Anthony.

"They said that they were Agents of Chaos. What did they mean?"

"It means that the next great war is coming." Anthony turned his eyes from the sky above to Su.

"The next great war, like the one that the races all fought together, side by side?"

"Yeah, that's the one."

"I thought that it was nothing but an old story, one that those who didn't want to fight used to try to fight back." Su accepted what Anthony said. He had fought humans for his entire life, but he had come to trade with them and learned that they were not all bad; it was just that people could be led astray.

"This war has been going on for a long time. It involves all of the people of Dena, for it's very soul. The Agents of Chaos work to infiltrate our homes, our cities and create chaos, to disrupt us and turn us against one another so that they can devour Dena and exterminate us," Anthony said.

Su thought on the state of Dena. Two of the most populous races were in a war against each other, although there had been a break in the fighting for the last three years. *It is only a matter of time until one side finds a reason to attack the other.*

"So this war right now?"

"I'm not sure but I think that the Agents of Chaos are behind it. They might also be behind the reason that there aren't any more Guardians and only a few people know about us. We're more of a myth than a reality." Anthony sounded as if he had more questions left unanswered. "We're stronger together than apart." Anthony turned to leave.

"Thank you," Su said.

Anthony looked back. "I just told you what you needed to hear, what your people needed to hear."

Anthony's voice made Su's heart twist. With his loss so recent, he could tell that he had experienced that same debilitating pain.

Su looked back up at the night sky, rubbing his leg that had been mangled. *Stronger together than apart. If they're the reason that this war has been going on for so long...* A chill ran down Su's spine, thinking of it. There had been times in the past where a peace could have been reached but then something had happened and stopped it from being established. Now they had been at war for so long that it was just a part of Dena.

***

"I meant to ask you earlier, but that bull familiar..." Su started.

"Ah, Bruce?" From Anthony's left arm, a green bull raised his head, looking out on the world. Instead of the anger that had been in his eyes before, they were clear as he looked at Su.

Su once again felt that bloodline suppression. "How is this possible?" Su asked.

Anthony looked confused and Su quickly covered up what he was thinking.

If someone learned that he had a familiar able to suppress our blood-lines, they might hunt him down. For it to be able to suppress my blood-line, even if we're not from the same bloodline, it must be a powerful familiar, closely related to the beast kin.

"Does he have intelligence?" Su asked, shocked by the light in the bull's eyes. His body turned brown slowly, but there were hints of green in his hair and his eyes shone like polished emeralds.

"He's plenty smart; he just doesn't speak common. Just communicates in other ways," Anthony said as Bruce left Anthony's arm. Bruce walked on the air as he circled around, before he went back into Anthony's arm.

"He's your familiar—is he a clan spirit?" Su asked.

"A clan spirit? That sounds familiar. *Heh*, familiar sounding familiar—that's a tongue twister!"

Su forced out a laugh as well, not sure what to say. "If I was you, I would be wary about letting others from the beast kin see Bruce."

"Oh?"

Su paused. If he had just met Anthony, he would have turned him over to the authorities. If he was keeping and controlling a clan spirit, it was a great dishonor if he had enslaved it, but seeing the two of them interact and Anthony's actions... *I couldn't see him forcing a clan spirit into submission.*

Su trusted his gut and let out a sigh and the tension that had built up within him. "Clan spirits are spirits that look over a clan. When we create our tattoos, we enhance the power that we can draw out from our bloodlines which extend back through our ancestors and the clan spirits. Clan spirits can combine with a beast kin, increasing their power greatly, but it is up to the spirit to choose who they want to combine with as they are tying themselves to the bodies of others. They can guide one's cultivation and increase their power in battle, training them constantly—a master inside of their head and their body, looking after them constantly."

Chapter: I Spy

The next morning, they left the campsite behind. They were all closer together, looking like a group once again.

Anthony, Aila, and Tommie rode in the back. They took their time; they were so close now they were only a few days from the city.

Anthony turned his head to the side as he heard something in the distance. "Are we expecting any kind of military around here?"

"What do you mean?" Gus asked.

"Can you hear that?"

Gus turn his head and focused on listening. "Everyone move to the side. Legion coming through!"

They reacted quickly. The carts shifted to the side as everyone looked around and started talking, advancing slower than before.

"Why would the legion be moving?" Anthony asked.

"There is a reserve training camp nearby. There wasn't supposed to be any military movements. I have my channels to make sure that we don't run into anything like this. So it must mean something happened..." Gus trailed off before reaching into his pack and pulling out his cloak. "You should put this on. They shouldn't do anything but they could arrest you and hold you for some time."

Anthony nodded and put the cloak on, hiding his armor.

"I'm going to head to the front and meet with the riders," Gus said. His bedar picked up his speed, meeting up with Su before continuing beyond the caravan.

They didn't have to wait long until they saw the scouts from the army. They were talking with Gus, who was bringing them back toward the caravan.

He waved Su over to meet with them. More scouts riding on their bedars could be seen in the forest on either side of the road, checking out the caravan and looking for threats.

The scouts in the forest continued on. The caravan was brought to a halt with Su's gesture and they moved farther off the road. He left with a scout, moving toward the approaching army that was hidden by the rolling hills.

"What should we do?" Aila asked Anthony in a low voice.

"We wait. We haven't done anything wrong and we have papers," Anthony said.

"Then why are you wearing that cloak?"

"Pretty stylish, no? Think of updating to a desert retro look—just need a scarf and some of those gnome goggles, roguish scars on my armor, a bit sandblasted. Badassery at its finest!"

Aila groaned. It looked as if Anthony was back to his same joke-filled self. She hid a smile. It was good to have him back. It made Dena seem less dark than before.

Su returned with Gus, heading for Aila, Tommie, and Anthony.

"I don't like this," Tommie said.

"Come on, Tommie. Stiff upper lip and all of that. This is how you build character," Anthony said from beneath his cloak.

Su and Gus looked nervous as they led a massive leader from the bull clan over. She had proud black horns that stuck out of the top of her well-cared-for helmet. Her eyes scanned over the people in the convoy, making most of them look away. Her guards moved with her, fanning around her more out of instinct that had been hammered into them after continuous fighting.

Her eyes fell on Anthony as her hand lowered to her blade.

Anthony felt Bruce stir.

"This young upstart is thinking about challenging me? She needs another dozen eons and a new spirit!"

"Bruce, don't create a scene."

"If she tries something, I'll act."

Bruce quieted down. He didn't leave but remained there, awake on his arm.

***

Commander Tysien was a large Elephant Kin. She surveyed the group before she looked at the man hiding underneath his cloak; he looked up at her and she thought that his eyes were glowing. She tightened her grip on the sword.

Filthy human. Hiding among these people. And the story about the Agents of Chaos—that must be a lie that they used in order to try to get him through Selenus. I'll get to the bottom of this. Can't trust a human. Even a child.

Memories she swore that she would never forget appeared in the back of her mind.

"Take off the hood," she said.

The knight did so, revealing his armored self underneath.

The other guards all looked at him warily, ready to draw their weapons as they circulated their bloodline.

She had fought beside them for a number of years; they moved as one, a group that had gone through life-and-death trials before.

"Papers?" she asked.

"Good morning. Nice day out, isn't it?" The man pulled out papers and passed them to her.

She nodded at the man and one of her guards moved his bedar closer, taking the papers and moving back to her.

She felt as though the whole caravan was looking at her.

"Commander." The guard passed her the papers.

She looked them over. They were all correct and they had the seal of the guard captain from Enni.

Being that close to the border, the city guard isn't going to be some simple-headed fool.

The little girl's face flashed behind her eyes and she made it appear as if she were reviewing the papers closer.

"All right, I'll need to check these closer. You and your companions will come with me and my guards back to Skalafell to check your identities and your papers. Convoy Leader Su, you and your people are free to go. Let's move!" She turned her bedar. He was a scarred older beast but there was a fierce look in his eyes; the other bedar moved back, feeling his power.

"Commander, this isn't really necessary. They saved our lives," Su said.

"So you have said. I will need a full report. I hope that you can have it to my office within the next day," Tysien said.

Su looked as if he wanted to say more, but he figured that it wasn't going to change anything.

"Yes, Commander," Su said with a dejected look on his face. He looked at the armored knight Anthony and his companions with an apologetic look.

The other members of the caravan looked annoyed as well, but they had the presence of mind to not voice their thoughts.

Her guards moved around Anthony and his companions, a gnome and an elf.

Are they all part of his cover? Do they know anything or not?

Anthony and his group followed after her as they were herded by her guards.

They moved over the hills and left the convoy behind.

Anthony and his companions talked. The gnome was nervous. The elf seemed as if she were on a sightseeing tour, acting as though everything were fine.

Anthony, on the other hand, seemed *bored.*

"I spy, with my little eye, something that begins with...*T*!"

"Tree?" the elf said in a tired voice.

"Nicely done! Your turn!"

"Pick something a little harder next time," the elf complained.

"All right, Miss Big Brains!" Anthony snorted and elbowed the air to his side, giving the guard there a look as if they knew what he meant.

They snarled at him and lowered their hands to their weapons.

"Doesn't make you bigger, threatening violence. Just means you're trying to compensate. Don't threaten violence, just attack—doesn't give them the time to react," Anthony said, disapprovingly.

Tysien looked back, her eyes carrying a hidden threat. The tension around their group increased, making one feel stifled.

"I spy, with my little eye, something beginning with *S*," the elf said.

Anthony looked ahead. "Skalafell?"

"Correct."

They crested a large hill. A plains stretched out ahead of them. Skalafell was a large city, with some eight hundred thousand residents. A river ran along it, providing shipping for the canals that ran up to the northeast, where Norlund lay, and then cut to the east and the west. East was the front lines; west was more cities and villages and then the coast.

On the road leading to the southeast, the road that they were on, one could see an entire legion moving out, forty thousand beast kin and five thousand bedar, with a long trailing supporting caravan following behind them.

They toted their colors high for the Skalafell legion, showing off each cohort's own flag.

Tysien's eyes drifted to the east where the camp lay, back from the river so it would be hard to be attacked from it, but close enough to receive and send supplies to the front lines. They had their own roads that curved around Skalafell to move troops if needed.

The camp was dull grays and browns, contrasting against the white walls and red roofing tiles of Skalafell. Boats raised their masts to catch the wind as they headed down the large locks, or drew them in as they got close to the city. One would need to know Skalafell well to see that the ships were all leaving or stopping in the middle of the river, away from the Skalafell docks.

While the city shone in the light, Tysien couldn't hear the familiar noise of work in the distance. Her heart felt heavy as they continued on, passing the legion marching down the road with grim looks on their faces.

Chapter: Skalafell's Secret

They headed toward the camp, passing one legion as another could be seen getting ready. There were carriages of supplies being pulled together and the leaders were yelling out to get everything in motion.

They crossed the river over a wooden drawbridge and then went up the hill into the camp.

"Camp Leader Jaclu wants to see you," one of the guards at the gate said.

Tysien nodded and looked behind her. "Take them to the holding cells." She urged her bedar forward into the camp. She moved through the open areas that were now filled with carts and members of the legion preparing to move out.

She reached the tallest building in the camp, riding with one foot as her bedar slowed down. She dropped off, handing her reins to the waiting guard in one fluid motion as she stepped forward, passing between the stone walls and heavyset wooden door.

She went up the stairs in the building, missing messengers who were rushing between rooms inside the building or passing orders to the people outside of the building's walls.

She reached out to knock on a door as it opened before her. A messenger dodged around her in a panic; then, seeing who it was, their face seemed to turn white.

She already ignored them and walked into the room.

"Commander Tysien!" Jaclu, the jaguar kin camp leader raised herself to her full height. She wasn't as tall as Tysien, but there was a power in her onyx eyes that made even Tysien tremble slightly.

"Reporting as ordered!" She rendered a salute and dropped to a knee.

"Reporting as you were found. We have a plague rampaging in Skalafell and we have to move out our forces so that they don't catch it as well and what were you doing?"

"I was moving with the departing legion to make sure that there were no issues as commanded, but there was a caravan coming toward Skalafell. They had an elf, a gnome, and a *human* among them."

Jaclu's eyes thinned as her ears lay lower along her head. "Did they have their papers?"

"They did," Tysien said, quickly speaking as she saw the change in Jaclu's eyes. "I thought it would be best that I bring them back here to question them and find out the validity of those papers. We were just hit with a plague—it is strange that there was a human found among them."

Jaclu turned to one of the messengers standing along the wall, not daring to move so it was easy to think of them as furniture.

"Bring them to me." Jaclu walked over to her desk.

The messenger saluted and ran out of the room at their top speed.

"I also got some news on the caravan. They said that there were cultists on the road from here to Enni, that they were saved by two people. I talked to the leader of the twelfth legion. I told him to investigate the place that the caravan talked about," Tysien said.

"Yet the first thing you report to me is a human who has papers, not the fact that there might be a cult working in our backyard. If this plague is the work of anyone, then it would need to be carried out by a group of people, like a cult. Not like three people. Are the gnome or elf enslaved?"

"Not that I know of. There were no markings on them or collars to show that they were." Tysien sensed her argument was falling apart, not because it wasn't valid, but because Jaclu was asking the wrong questions and leading her to the wrong answers.

"Do you have their papers?" Jaclu sat down and raised her hand.

Tysien stepped forward and pulled out the papers that she had tucked into her armor.

Jaclu took the papers and looked them over. "I served with Etheras. He is a good man. He wouldn't give these papers to anyone, even if his life was under threat." Jaclu put the papers on her desk. "Now, about these cultists—what did the elder of the caravan say?"

"They said that they were poisoned, some kind of sleeping concoction was added to their food. A new person joined their crew, a scout. It looks like there might have been something fishy that happened with their previous scout. They woke up in some kind of ritual; it drew power out of people and then poured it into others. The cultists said that they were part of a chaotic cult. The leader of the cult and the ritual had power leaking through his body. Wasn't like the elven magic or the human familiars or our tattoos, something different." Tysien paused as she saw recognition in Jaclu's eyes.

"The Agents of Chaos followers," Jaclu said.

"Yes," Tysien said.

Jaclu sighed. "When I was a young trainee, I was part of the Kreas camp. When the mutiny happened, there were people in their ranks saying that they were followers of the Agents of Chaos. They used magic to blind people, to bring them into illusions. They would fight their allies with a smile on their face. People said that it was a mutiny but it was the cultists. They were hunted down. We thought that they were all dead, but then there has been more and more rumors of them in the last couple of years and signs of them here and there in different ways. If there is a fight or strange happenings, it is either an anomaly or people who follow the Agents of Chaos. They say that the Agents of Chaos are not from Dena; they are coming to change the balance of power, and they are powerful. The ones with the glowing changing power within their bodies are incredibly strong and can twist nature itself and stain Dena when they use their power, changing their very bodies and what they are." Jaclu's eyes focused once again as she seemed to realize just where she was and what she was doing.

"Take anything that is related with them seriously," Jaclu said, looking at Tysien deeply.

"Yes, Camp Leader," Tysien said.

"Tell Commander Yisnus to investigate the ritual site reported by the caravan with a group of intermediaries."

A messenger stepped out and saluted. They ran out of the door, right into a Gnome, Elf and a Knight who had to dodge to the side to make way for the messenger.

"Damn, this place is busy," the knight muttered.

Tysien raised her guard seeing the human knight.

"Come in," Jaclu said.

The door opened. Tysien's guards were there with the gnome, the elf, and the human between them.

"Morning, Camp Leader—well, more of an afternoon here. So, when did the plague start?" The knight walked into the room.

"Who told you about the plague?" Jaclu asked.

"You did, just now. I thought that people are looking at the city as if there is something to fear. The ports are closed and there are no people leaving the city. Looks like there are groups of guards around the entrances into the city. So if you're not keeping people out—you would have kept the legions here to defend it—then you must be keeping something in. Usually sickness, or some kind of rebellion. No news of friction in Skalafell, so..." The man shrugged. "Plague."

"It seems like you're rather observant..." Jaclu paused, waiting for the man to fill in his name.

"Anthony. This is Aila Wranoris and Tommie, son of Todd. Really big *t* lovers—the letter, not the drink. Do you drink tea?" Anthony asked.

"Once in a while," Tommie started when Jaclu frowned. "B-but you know, I am really thinking that I should drink more of it. Lots of health benefits, I've heard, you know!" he said with an ingratiating smile.

"What is your reason for being here?" Jaclu asked Anthony.

"A grand adventure. You see, it started in the north—"

"We got a task from the high elves. We need to head to Ilsal. We're passing through to one of the port towns to get a boat to the islands." Aila cut him off.

"Any other plans?"

"I was wondering what your plan is to deal with the plague. I don't see any of your healers going in there," Anthony asked.

"Anthony," Aila said in a warning tone.

"What? It's just a question. The way it looks, they're just closing off the city and hoping for the best," Anthony said.

"I'd suggest that you continue on your trip." Jaclu held out the papers for Tysien.

She took them and passed them to Aila.

"Thank you," Aila said.

Jaclu waved to the guards and they moved aside. The trio looked around and started to leave.

"The Agents of Chaos," Jaclu said in a light voice.

Anthony's demeanor changed as he looked back at Jaclu. "Was this their doing?"

"I'm not sure. Do you think so?" Jaclu's eyes locked onto him.

"It's possible. Where there is one rat, there will be others. It is clear that they have some strength in this area to try to capture a convoy that is travelling from a frontline town to a city with a legion training camp outside of it."

"What do they want?" Jaclu asked.

"I think you know that already," Anthony said.

"What do you think of them?"

"I think that there are many people who can be saved, but there are some who are too far gone."

"And what happens to those people?"

"There's nothing that can be done for them. Though it's different for the people in the city. I hope that you help out the people in the city. It isn't their fault that there is a plague," Anthony said, changing the subject.

"We only have limited resources here. If our people get the plague, then how are they to fight?" Jaclu said.

Anthony let out a tired sigh. "Just what happened while I was gone—more scared of each other than willing to help their own."

Tysien could just barely hear his whisper and she felt sadness in his words. She frowned slightly. *He probably said it quietly so that I would hear it and then I would think that he could be trusted. I can't let my guard down. I'll make sure to watch him closely. He's dangerous.*

"Have a good day, Camp Leader Jaclu, Commander Tysien." Anthony turned and the rest of his group joined him. His cloak moved behind him as he closed the door.

Jaclu was quiet for a moment. "Tysien, watch him. I don't think that he is here to cause any issues but he's strong and opinionated—that makes him dangerous."

"Yes, Camp Leader," Tysien said.

***

"So, what are we going to do now?" Aila asked.

"Well, we are about a week's ride from the coast," Tommie said.

"We're going to help out the people of Skalafell," Anthony said.

Aila nodded, as if she expected that answer.

"How?" Tommie asked.

"I'll work to see if we can get the support of the traders outside of the city and try to get some support from the military," Aila said.

"I'll go into the city. It's not like I can get sick anyway. Tommie, I'll need you to make devices that stop people from contracting the plague—masks, soap, clean water," Anthony said. "I want you to find out as much as you can about the plague, anything and everything. See what the soldiers think. See if there is anyone there who would be willing to help out, if in a non-official capacity."

Tommie relaxed a bit and nodded.

"If the city is closed, how are you going to get inside?"

"Jump? Probably jump," Anthony said.

Aila remained in the camp while Tommie headed opposite, to the lake where traders had put up some tents and some of the sailors who had been intending to head into Skalafell had moored their boats close to.

Anthony walked toward the city. Legionnaires acted as guards. Their expressions were grim and dark as they gave Anthony threatening looks.

How would you feel about standing guard over a city that might have people you know inside it and they're suffering through a plague?

Anthony kept on walking. He moved up toward the city, circling it.

He took off at a run, crossing the ground quickly. He jumped upward and his fingers dug in the wall. He kept on running, using his initial momentum to get higher before he grabbed the top of the battlements and hauled himself up onto the walkway.

He crouched down. The walls were emptied. Inside the wall, he could see the city. Very few people moved on the streets. Most of them looked at one another with suspicion, with dark looks in their eyes as they scurried from place to place.

"Come on, Solomon. Let's take a closer look." Black mist wrapped up his leg and covered his entire body. He fell off the wall silently, falling into the shadows below as he flitted around the city, unseen and unheard.

He looked into windows and saw those who were able to, looking after those who were affected. Their skin was pale, their body covered in sweat as they fought an inner battle for survival.

"Poor bastards," Anthony muttered. He kept moving past the windows, seeing families coming together, trying everything they could to help those affected. Mothers, fathers, brothers, sisters, daughters, sons, and grandparents: the plague didn't care. It had spread like wildfire through the city.

"This is the doing of the gods! We must repent to seek salvation!"

"And then there are the people looking to take control of this or see it in a different light." Anthony sighed as he saw people giving sacrifices to their household gods or to their clan spirits in an effort to help their loved ones. People offered cures: some were real and some weren't. Others were taking advantage of the city being shut down. The guards and the city lord weren't unaffected, so there were few patrols; most stores had been closed up and left alone as the people who owned and worked at them had gone home.

So these enterprising few were starting to look at breaking into different stores and looting what they could from them.

All of this fell into Anthony's eyes or were whispered into his ear as Solomon's shadows spread across the city, creating a net that would allow Anthony to know everything that happened.

"If this is the work of the Agents of Chaos, then we will be able to root them out, though they're good at hiding. If it is just a plague, then I'll have to work hard to make sure that law and order doesn't break down and work to try to save as many people as possible."

Solomon got his attention. He wasn't capable of speech like Bruce yet but Anthony could understand what he meant.

Anthony, who had been hiding in an alleyway, stood and started to use the walls of the alleyway to get higher.

Dave's golden light, looking like a serpent's scaled body, wrapped around Anthony's body as he jumped up. The golden power condensed on Anthony's back, turning into a pair of golden glass-like wings. Anthony shot forward, using Dave's enhancement to allow him to fly and glide for a short distance.

***

He heard a woman crying, sobbing and pleading for help.

Anthony ran across rooftops and glided between buildings, Skalafell blurring beneath him. He reached the lady who was crying out.

Her baby was covered in angry red patches and was coughing out, its face turning blue.

Anthony jumped and spun, making it through the bedroom window.

The woman clutched her baby closer as Anthony held up his hands.

"I'm here to help." He saw the fear in her eyes, as if he were the reaper who would take her baby's life.

She only clutched the baby, whose coughing only got worse, tighter.

Anthony was in a panic. "Do you want your baby to live?" he yelled.

"Help! Help! Someone is trying to—!"

Anthony cast Words of Truth on her.

"Yes, help Jole, please!"

Anthony started to move his hands as he drew in power from the surrounding area. *"Bruce, going to need your help here."*

"You have it."

Anthony drew a spell out in the air. Green lines connected together into a spell formation before it shot forward and landed on little Jole's chest.

It rested there as healing energies entered the little baby's chest.

"Hmm, there is a plague here, but then there is a curse hidden inside. The plague can be healed, but the curse will need to be absolved. Would need to get a priest to do that, or find out what the curse is and destroy it," Bruce said to Anthony.

"With curses, if we don't get it correct then it can backfire and kill the person. Will healing the baby affect the curse?" Anthony asked quickly.

"The plague weakens the body; the curse increases the damage and makes it nearly impossible to wipe away the plague. It will come back.

Healing those affected will remove the plague from their bodies, and relieve the symptoms somewhat, but it is only prolonging the inevitable." Bruce's gruff voice sounded pained.

Little Jole's appearance started to improve. He started crying out again in his mother's arms as the dots on his body died down.

Someone had to have done this deliberately. No plague would have a curse component in it naturally.

The mother checked her son, relief etched into her expression. "Thank you," she said, overwhelmed with emotions. She didn't know what else to say.

There was the sound of a door slamming open and footsteps rang on the stairs.

"Anya! Jole!" a scared and heart-stricken voice called out.

Anya turned toward the door. "Davin!" she yelled out as the door burst open. She looked back to where Anthony had been standing but he wasn't there anymore.

"Are you okay? I heard you yelling out." Davin's face twisted in pain, expecting the worst.

"No, no, everything is okay," Anya said.

Anthony stood on the roof of the house. He jumped off, wings extending from his back as he took off.

"A guardian angel was looking after us," she said.

Anthony felt stifled. *I was only able to slow the progress of the plague, not stop it.*

***

Keze had snuck out of her house. Her father was too sick to do anything and all of the servants had been released to go home, other than those who were part of their household. While the others were getting sick, she remained healthy.

The plague had always been something that her mother said to her in warning and that adults talked about with grave voices. She had been too young to care. Now she saw how much they were in pain, how tired her mother was from running the city and looking after her husband. Her father, a man Keze had always seen as this strong figure, was now unable to move from bed, wasting away before her eyes.

With so few people around, it hadn't been hard for her to sneak out. She needed to do something. The healing concoctions that they had were running low and she knew that there was a healer in the tradesman district. She was going to go and look for him to get a cure for her father.

She wore a cloak to hide her features. As she moved along the streets, people looked at her with suspicion. She was used to being stared at, so she only picked up her pace, wanting to get to the healer.

She knew the city like the back of her hand. From a young age, she had spent her time looking at the maps of the city, getting to know all of the different streets, the alleyways, the stores and stalls. When she had gone out in her carriage with her father, he had asked her where they were, how to get to another place in the city, and how to get back home. It turned into a sort of game.

Now she could only bite her lip as she thought about how happy she had been to see him laughing and praising her. She had only seen him laugh and be happy when he was with her or her mother. To everyone else, he was cold and unreachable, standing above them.

If I can get him to laugh again, to give me a hug, and I can tell him how much he worried me... When he gets up, I'll bug him about how much he scared me and get him to get me ice cream, buckets and buckets of it.

Her heart warmed, not at thinking of the ice cream, but seeing his face, that smile that lit up her heart, and being hugged in those strong and reliable arms.

She picked up her pace. As she went down the alleyway, she heard shuffling on the rooftops. *Birds, scaring me like that!* She calmed her heart and she kept on moving.

A shadow jumped over the wall and dropped in front of her. It was a man. He wore rags across his body; they were dark and stained—hard worked and hard washed—and patched together many times. His mouth was covered, as was his fur and body. But his claws were extended, making him someone from one of the feline clans.

She turned to find two others had dropped from the roofs behind her.

Panic took her as she looked at them, thinking of the fears that her mother had put into her mind, telling her what would happen if someone with bad intentions was able to get ahold of her.

Keze grabbed her cloak and pulled it tighter around her, as if it would ward off the three attackers.

"Give us your concoctions!" the feline man in front said.

"I-I don't have any," Keze said, trying to fight the fear and the tremor in her voice.

"Look at you—out here with your fine clothes and jewels, walking as if there is nothing wrong. We know you nobles are hiding the cures," one of the men behind her said. He had to be from the bear clans based on his size, girth, and the claws that protruded from his hand. The other looked to be from the reptile clan, with their thin body and the way that the cloth over their mouth moved as their tongue had to be moving underneath.

"We might be poor but we're not blind. Look at you—perfectly healthy, even with all of the plague going on. What did you take to heal you?" the bear asked.

"They must've started it, like the rumors said," the reptile said.

The feline's claws extended more. "Give us your concoctions or tell us how to cure the plague. There is no one around to help you and we don't want to hurt you."

"I don't have any concoctions. I don't know how to cure it. Please don't hurt me. My father is sick and I want to go to the healer in the trade district to see if I can get a cure from him." Tears ran down her face, fear gripping her. She could feel death wrapping around her back like a cold embrace, calling out to her, promising to take her away from this.

She had been scared before: scared for getting caught doing something she knew she shouldn't be doing, or now when she saw her father withering away and her mother having to work so hard and then crying in her study when she didn't think anyone was looking.

This was a new kind of scared as she felt her life hanging in the balance between these three's decisions.

There was the sound of wings; she barely noticed it but the feline's headdress moved as their ears twitched around.

"What is that?"

As the sun was going down, the shadows were hard to see through, making it hard to see in the sky.

There was the sound of wings being folded away as a new shadow dropped from the sky between the reptile and the bear. With two strikes, the shadow moved, knocking out the bear and the reptile. The force of the blows made them hit the walls on either side as the man shot forward. Keze saw the armored man as he pushed her to the side and grabbed the feline's hand as he moved past. Using their armor and his body, he threw the feline man into the wall, making them let out a painful breath. The man grabbed them and tossed them down the alleyway, between the two others.

"Damn, seems like I've still got it," the knight said, giving Keze a thumbs-up.

She gave him a thumbs-up in return.

"Don't worry, little miss. You're all okay. I just need to talk to these three right here," the knight said.

Keze nodded. It all happened so fast she didn't know what to think.

He stepped past her and she saw his cloak moving. She could see a faint tree on his back. The branches were brown, with hints of gold; the leaves a brilliant green as it seemed to move with the breeze, capturing one's attention and making their mind calm down.

"All right you three, for attempting to mug someone else, threatening violence in a time of chaos, and disturbing the peace, I punish you with community service in this time of need."

The bear started to get up as the shadows behind him moved and chains looped around his body, holding him down.

"They're killing us and you want to defend them! You—!" The bear's head seemed to have cleared enough for him to see just who their attacker was.

"Human?" His word came out like a cold whisper, like a cold bucket of water on the two others and Keze.

She had seen humans from afar—a few traders who came down from the coast—but she was never allowed to meet one in person. She was in a high position; if they were able to capture her, she could be used to pressure her parents.

Now she studied the man. A new fear gripped her, one that had been instilled in her by her parents. She no longer felt safe around this human, thinking of the cruel things that she had heard that they had done. She remembered the expressions on her father and her mother's faces when they had talked to her about humans who had attacked their people, sold them into slavery, that ravaged their cities and that had started this bloody war that had claimed countless lives.

She *knew* that they were bad people, people who would use and destroy others to push their own gains. They were sneaky and they were cunning, filled with lies and deceit. How could someone who had to use the strength of others and the familiars be noble or right?

Without knowing it, a sneer had appeared on her face as she looked at this man.

He must know who I am, looking down on me and trying to use me to turn against the people of the city. Does he want to use me as a hostage?

"Been that way for a few hundred years and aim to do so for a few hundred more. Do you have a defense?" the human asked.

"A defense?" the feline asked.

"Just kill us, you coward!" the reptile hissed out.

Their clothes had been skewed so Keze could now see more details of their faces. These were younger men, ones who showed signs of hard work and labor.

"I do not kill unless absolutely necessary, my dear reptilian friend," the man said in an amicable voice as a pressure weighed down on everyone and then dissipated, making one feel relaxed. "Now, *why* did you attempt to mug her?" The Knight asked.

"She's a noble—they're hoarding all of the medicines," the feline burst out.

The others nodded.

"Our families and the people we care about are sick. We wanted to help out. We knew that the nobles had to have stuff to help them. We didn't have a plan—we just wanted to do *something*," the reptile said.

"We were around the castle, looking to see if there was any way to get medicine to help out our families. Then we saw her moving through the streets. There's no way anyone but a noble would have a cloak like that, with silver and gold thread and fine silks," the feline said.

"We didn't mean her any harm. It was just—with her refusing that they had any kind of cure and her being perfectly healthy—we're not dumb, just poor and weak. She was looking down on us." The bear dropped his head, ashamed.

The would-be muggers all looked at the ground in shame.

"We just wanted to help our families," the feline said.

"Your reasons are good, but still, if you let your emotions take you away, as our bear clan friend said here, you could've hurt someone. What do you think that the nobles would have done if you had hurt one of their children?"

"They'd have come after us with everything that they have," the reptile said after some long seconds.

I just wanted to get something for my father. Keze started to see how shortsighted her goals had been. *I should've told Mother, or got some guards to come with me. Maybe they would have told me to wear clothes that weren't so easy to identify, or sent a messenger out to the healer.* Keze's head was a mess.

"Your judgement stands. You will be drafted as emergency members of the Skalafell relief and crisis team. Throughout this time, you will help and assist the people of Skalafell." Purple runes appeared around the men's wrists and latched onto them.

Slave collars! Just what kind of monster is he? Keze, who had been edging away, now turned and fled, running as fast as she could down the corridor.

"Little miss, make sure you go home!" the man yelled after her, making her run even faster.

She ran as fast as she could, dropping to all fours. Her mother had told her to never do it, but now she needed the speed as she ran no different from a cat, ripping her dress in the process.

People watched her go by as she ran through the streets, before running into a patrol.

Seeing them, she nearly fell apart in relief. Her heart had been through so much she didn't know what to say to them as the leader of the patrol looked at her in alarm.

"Little Miss Keze, what are you doing out here? What happened? Form up! Defend the city lord's daughter!"

The guards all moved around her as the guard captain checked on her and then picked her up, all of them moving toward the city lord's castle.

***

The three men had a dull look on their faces as they touched the collar around their wrists, looking as if their life were over.

"Slavers," the reptile spat.

"Okay, so the first order of business: we need to know how affected people are, so you three will need to recruit people into our ranks and go door to door to talk to the people, see how they are, how their families are," Anthony said.

The three of them looked at the ground.

"Eyes up *here*!" Anthony's eyes flashed green for a moment. Bruce appeared on his arm, snorting and looking at the trio, putting pressure on them through their bloodlines.

The three were startled as they looked up at him.

"I have taught hundreds of beast men and I have fought beside thousands of you. I have called many of you my brothers and my sisters. I will save as many people in Skalafell as I can, if it is the last damned thing that I do. If you dare to get in my way or you look to shirk your duties, then you are *useless* to me. What you do here will decide the fate of your loved ones. It will decide the fate of Skalafell. The longer we mess around here over our differences, the more people will die. Do I make myself *perfectly* clear?" His voice rang out with the punctuality of a training officer.

"Sir," the bear answered.

"If you do as you say, we'll agree," the feline said.

The reptile nodded, agreeing with the feline.

"That is fair. Now, we need to know how many people are affected and the severity. Do you know the stages of the plague?"

"They cough some, get wheezy, then really tired. Then the cold sweats and these red bumps appear," the feline started.

"Scales are shed and their hair falls out," the reptile added.

"Then they waste away into nothing—they go not long after," the bear said, his voice bitter and annoyed.

"Okay so, tired and cold sweats stage one; red bumps, scales and fur falling off stage two; and death stage three. Categorize people according to that. Gather as many people as possible to go house to house, check on their neighbors and the like. Also, we need to know the condition of their food and water. As we go on, we will collect food from people and disperse it out as needed, as well as water. What are your names?"

"Mai," the reptile said.

"Jun," the feline said.

"Ubi," the bear said.

"Okay, Jun, you go and check on the different wells. I want to know their condition and how much water they have. Mai, go and talk to your friends and see how many you can recruit to help us. Ubi, start going door to door and make a system for categorizing the people and their need for food and water. Mai, as you get more people, send a third of them to Jun to check the wells, and the rest to Ubi." Anthony turned his head to the side as Solomon warned him that there was another crime being committed.

"Get to work. Do not hurt others unless they are going to hurt you and help out those you see in need. Make sure to cover your mouths and noses—it'll protect you from the plague more."

"How will we get the information to you?" Jun asked.

"In the square near the south gate, the one that has the legionnaire's memorial in it—on the eastern wall, there will be a marking like this." Anthony showed his Guardian emblem, making sure that they all saw it. "Place your notes on it and new orders will appear on the wall," Anthony said. "If you have people who don't have a job, send them to the wall and they will be given a new job. Don't fail this city."

With that, Anthony ran past them and over their heads. They turned, seeing the tree on his back as Dave's wings spread out from his back. He jumped into the sky with the setting sun and shot across the city.

Solomon had spread over the city like a net, but he was only able to communicate short ideas to Anthony. He needed more information and people to help him. First he needed to stabilize Skalafell, to arrest those trying to or those who had committed a crime; then he would use them to affect change in Skalafell.

"Two birds with one stone." Anthony soared over Skalafell. The city now fell under his jurisdiction; he watched over every alleyway and every major road. Solomon was being strained to his limit, but as Anthony had been awake for longer, his power was starting to return; one could see this with his ability to materialize Dave's wings and awaken Bruce.

In the square he had talked about, shadows converged together to form a black Guardian symbol that looked over the square. The eye seemed to look at everyone who passed as they scurried away.

Underneath the eye, words appeared, marking an area for jobs and an area for information.

Anthony dropped from the sky, using Dave's wings with one burst of strength to arrest his fall. He landed in front of a young member of the rhino clan.

"Ah, look out! Sorry about this." Anthony punched them in the face.

The "young" rhino was still massive. His eyes rolled back up into his head as he fell backward, making a dull noise.

"Ouch." Anthony passed them and headed into the store. The little bell rung as he opened the door. "Ah, I do like a cute little doorbell—though, looters, not so much," Anthony said as several people looked at him, all with sacks in their hands as they stuffed goods into their bags.

"Get him!"

"Time to go to work!" Anthony stretched out his gauntlets as he met the first attacker with a kitchen blade. He grabbed their arm that they'd extended out as if their arm were a spear.

"First knife fight, I'm assuming." Anthony hit their knee and then punched them in the face, making them see stars.

They cried out in pain, falling on the ground and holding their broken nose as they forgot about the knife that Anthony kicked, sticking into a wall.

Two more came at Anthony. Their bodies were too big in the smaller space, making them crash into each other. Anthony dodged to the side and tripped one, sending them into the other. They went down in a mess of limbs, now trying to make sure that they didn't accidentally stab each other.

Anthony started to whistle as he administered jabs and kicks to the uninitiated. Against these untrained looters, he just had to use the small shop around him, making it hard for them to move and get away from his attacks. He used the least amount of force to knock them out or leave them with a rather painful, but superficial, wound that hurt them enough to stop fighting.

"Hmm, real Timarea jerky. Ah, I wish I had taste buds still." Anthony sighed as he held a package. One attacker's blade went past his head, sticking into the wood of the cupboard. Anthony punched them in the jaw, sending them stumbling back and releasing their blade before he sent a kick right between their legs. The others on the floor in pain all winced as the kangaroo kin looked at Anthony, tilting his head; he went pale and dropped to the floor, letting out a pained groan filled with suffering.

"You can tuck them in but not that far." Anthony pat the kangaroo's head and walked past him, wincing even though they couldn't see his expression.

Right in the cajones! Ugh, sorry, dude!

Anthony cleared his throat as he looked at all of them on the floor, some trying to get back up. "All right, you lot, listen up! I accuse you of looting, trespassing on another's property without their permission, as well as breaking and entering, threatening violence in a time of chaos, and disturbing the peace. You could have really hurt someone with your kitchen appliances! How do you plead?"

"Guilty," their voices all called out. They looked at one another, not sure where that answer had come from.

"Very well, then I will punish you with community service in this time of need. You will put back this store how it was exactly and repair any damage. You will have to tip everyone who you buy items from ten percent for the next two years. If they do not accept it, then you will have to give that money to a charity of your choosing."

Anthony cast his binding and collars appeared on them all. "Now, you three will report to a fella called Jun."

***

"What are you doing?" a legionnaire asked as Tommie rooted around in the campfire.

"Ah!" Tommie nearly jumped out of his skin as he looked at the legionnaire and his five friends with him, all holding onto their weapons.

"I'm sorry—I am getting the charcoal and the animal fat from the fire!"

"What do you need that for, gnome?"

"Well, if I put them together, then I can use it to make a kind of soap." Tommie looked at his feet awkwardly.

"What do you need soap for?" The legionnaire's eyes thinned.

"Well, for the people in Skalafell—see if I can make soap and then toss it over the wall. Then my friend can get the soap into the people's hands and then they can use that and the masks that I make to try to stop the plague from spreading."

"You really mean to send it to the people in Skalafell?" the legionnaire asked.

"Yes." Tommie felt like an idiot underneath the gazes of these massive beast men.

"All right." The legionnaire retracted his gaze and looked to one of his men. "Stone Cut, you go and get some of the legionnaires to collect the charcoal and the animal fat together. Gnome, how do we make it into soap?"

"Well, it won't be real soap, but if you mix water, charcoal, and animal fat together, then it will at least make a soap-like substance," Tommie said.

"All right, Jorah, you get some boys to help to make the soap. Gnome, you teach him and he'll look after it. Now, you said something about masks?"

"Yeah, like cloth to put over your face so that it is harder for people to get infected. I was also going to make a water system that allows one to filter the water—would need to have some cloth and then a lot of the charcoal that has been burned, then rocks and sand," Tommie said.

"Conway, go to the stores and see if we have any cloth we're not using. Rinzen, get a party together—go and see if you can round up some people to get gravel and sand from the river. Anything else?"

"Uh, no," Tommie said.

"Good." The legionnaire looked to the others. "Move it, and get others to help. The next legion leaves in a day. They can sleep when they march."

The group with him moved off at a run.

"I'm Centurion Raul. Tell me how to make these different systems and I can teach my people," Raul said.

"Yes, but why?"

"Why teach me?" Raul asked in a dangerous voice.

"No, why are you helping me?" Tommie asked, not sure where he got the confidence to ask that question.

"Those are my people in Skalafell. I might not be a citizen of the city, but I spent my free time there quite a bit and we swore in the legion to protect our people. I have orders that I can't go into the city, to make sure that no one comes out. Instead of helping them, we're keeping them caged up. I understand why—we're in a state of war—but I still want to do something. If your friend is inside, I hope that he can get these resources to the people who need it. I don't care if he is making some money on the side, but if he takes too much and doesn't get this out to the people, then I will get into that city and cut him down," the centurion said.

Tommie couldn't help but laugh. The centurion looked at him, cocking his head to the side.

"Don't worry, Centurion. He's the last person to charge anyone money. I don't think he has a copper to his name and all he wants to do is help out is all."

Centurion Raul took a measure of Tommie before he walked forward. "I hope he is as you say. Now, how do we make these contraptions of yours?"

***

"And he just jumped up the wall into the city?" Jaclu asked Tysien.

"Yes, Camp Leader. I am looking for permission to follow him into the city. There is no knowing what he is doing in there." Tysien saluted as a messenger ran into the camp leader's room with a report.

"Speak," Jaclu said.

"Centurion Raul has mobilized some of the legion to gather charcoal, unused cloth, animal fat, sand, and gravel to assist a gnome," the messenger said.

"For what purpose?"

"He is looking to make materials that will aid the people inside Skalafell. The gnome is using the materials to make masks, soap, and water filtration items."

"Interesting. Do we have a report on the elf?" She looked to one of her aides.

They flipped open a notebook. "She headed into the trader camps that are opposite Skalafell with the gnome. They met up with some of the people from the caravan that they were with. She stayed with them and the gnome returned to raid the fires around the main camp. It looked like they were gathering food and creating food packages to send into the city. She is still in the trader camp currently and coordinating with them."

"Here are my suggestions." Jaclu looked around the room. Her orders stopped her from being able to do anything to help the people in the city, even if she wanted to do everything in her power to help them.

"I would want the stores to look at the food that we currently have and look at what we would need to have two months' worth of food, at a ration and a half per person. Then the excess to be checked for how fresh it is. We don't want food that would go bad in our storehouses. Also, Centurion Raul has the right idea. The legionnaires have been antsy as of recently. Make sure that they clean up the fires, and dig up some gravel and sand as exercise. At night, it has been chilly so we should get some fires going to keep everyone warm." Her eyes fell on the people in the room before she pointed at two messengers. "You go to the stores—you go to the traders." She looked back at the messenger who had come back. "You talk to Centurion Raul and pass on my thoughts; make sure that if he wants to carry out this punishment detail, he will have to command it. Tysien, I will okay your request to go into Skalafell. We need reports on what is happening in there in case there are any issues and to make sure that any donations that are sent in are given to the people who need it."

"I will not let you down." Tysien's heart that had been tight, unable to help the people in Skalafell, released a little bit. She was still wary of Anthony, but he and his people had given her an excuse to go into the city. *Just what are they trying to do? With our people looking after the supplies now, there will be no way for them to pass anything secretive to him. They might have been trying to use this as a way to smuggle items in and out of the city. I'll make sure that they're not trying to harm the people of Skalafell.*

"Everyone go and take a break—get some water. Tysien and I need to catch up on some private matters," Jaclu said.

The people cleared out of the room quickly and closed the door behind them. Jaclu's aides stood guard.

Jaclu pulled out a bag and put it on her desk. "These are concoctions that we have in our stores. Take these and use them on the city lord—see if any of them work. If they do, then I can give you the concoctions. It won't be enough to save them all but it'll save a lot of them. If none of them do, then we can only keep the quarantine. I have been authorized to use deadly force if people try to break out of the city."

Tysien took the bag from Jaclu, feeling the weight of the bag as she made sure to secure it to her hip tightly.

"This Anthony might actually be doing some good. Don't let your past experiences cloud your judgement. Who could know that the girl you saved would turn against you and unlock the gates to the camp?" Jaclu said.

Tysien's body burned in shame and anger, remembering the girl's smile as she opened the doors, the familiar cavalry of the humans storming into the castle, killing and destroying those around her. She had trusted the little girl, looked after her and felt like a mother to her. But her feelings had been wrong: she had brought in one of the humans' own, who had used her.

She saw Tysien as nothing more than a pawn, a piece to be played to destroy the beast kin. She had seen the hatred in the little girl's eyes, her mad laughter as the cavalry charged in with their blades.

"Burn and kill! Destroy them all! Take my hatred, beasts! Taste your own treatment!"

Tysien still had so many questions for her. *Why did she lead the attack against us? Just what was wrong with her to take so much joy in killing us all?*

She touched her chest, where she had been cut down. Some of the legionnaires made it out and took her with them. *Now she stands as one*

*of the Church of Light's chief judicators—Saintess Letanya, the youngest
saintess among the humans.*

"Yes, Camp Leader." Tysien forced the words out.

Jaclu only sighed. "You have your orders."

Tysien saluted, with Jaclu returning the salute. Tysien opened the doors and headed out into the camp and toward Skalafell.

***

Keze ran into her mother's arms, still wearing her tattered dress and cloak as she cried in her embrace.

Tissis couldn't keep up her anger. Her husband was affected by the plague, withering away no matter what treatment they gave him. Seeing Keze, all of her anger reached its limit but her hug stopped her from releasing it.

"I wanted to help Poppa but then when I was going to the healers, there were these men with claws and they wanted me to heal them but I didn't have the cure but they wouldn't listen. Then this human, a bad human, came in and enslaved them so I was scared and I ran away. He was wearing this armor and he beat them up!"

Keze's words were distorted but Tissis got enough of an idea.

"Find me this human and the three who attacked my daughter this minute!" she yelled. Her voice carried through the room. Everyone could feel her bloodline's power surging through her, as if she were bare seconds from putting on her own armor and searching the streets for these people herself as she gave vent to the helplessness and anger within her chest.

People rushed into action and all of the able-bodied guards were ordered out of their homes, leaving their loved ones behind as they scoured through the city, looking for the people who attacked the little miss.

As they went through the streets, their anger at the four people who took them away from their homes changed as they learned about the emergence of the Black Rags.

"What?"

Tissis was in her husband's office, looking at the guard captain.

"They're called the Black Rags. They're going around the city. They use their Black Rags to cover their faces. We thought that they were bandits and looters at first, but they're checking on the wells, seeing how full they are. Others are going house to house to see what the condition of people is. Some are making more masks to try to stop the spread of disease; others are drawing water up from the well and boiling it to purify the water and deliver it to different families. Those who are sick are being organized into different areas. Large warehouses have been cleared out and turned into medical facilities to try to isolate the plague."

"Who ordered them to do this?"

"There was a man, a knight, who supposedly told a bunch of them to do this, said that they were paying for their crimes by doing community service. Most of them have these purple chains around their wrists. Though more people are joining them. They answer to a wall that has this strange symbol on it. They go up and put their paper to the wall; there is a change on the wall and the information is added, possibly. Then they go to another part of the wall that says jobs. Either it creates a new job for them, or they're sent to report to someone to help them out."

Tissis had an uneasy feeling as the guard captain pulled out a piece of paper.

"This is a drawing of the image."

She took a look at it. "I have seen this before." She frowned and pinched the bridge of her nose. She leaned back in her chair. Her brain was just so tired. She was so tired.

She opened her eyes a few times to try to wet them.

She stood and turned around, looking at the painting. It was of a great battle, some unknown enemy and a group of people running into battle. Above it, there was a saying:

"May your judgement be heavy as it weighs the lives and souls of those under you." She read out the saying as her eyes looked at the top of the painting. There was the same shield, with an all-seeing eye in the middle of it.

I've seen this painting a thousand times and glanced at that symbol. She looked down at the image in her hand. *Does this mean something? It has to. No human has been in this room as long as my husband has ruled. So how would they know to do this? Is this one of the families playing for power? Even if they are to do so, there is no way that they can control the city.*

She was filled with more questions than answers.

"Come with me." She grabbed a scarf out of the drawer and she wrapped it around her face.

The guard captain followed her as she marched through the halls toward her family's private quarters.

She went through the doors before signaling to the guard captain. "You might want to put on a scarf," she said.

He pulled out some cloth from his belt and put it around his mouth and nose.

They passed another set of doors. There were guards wearing her family's crest; all of them wore masks as they stopped and bowed to her as she passed.

She got to a door where there were servants wearing masks, getting fresh clothes, food, and water. She passed them and entered her and her husband's room.

They walked across the room. Her husband lay down in their bed, covered in sweat. A thick medicinal smell hung in the air as herbs were being burned to try to cover the smell and help him recover.

She grimaced and moved her nose around at the smell as she moved closer to him.

He was covered in sweat and panting. As a member of the wolf clan, it was hard for him to cool down.

She sat next to him. As he felt the weight on the bed, he cracked open an eye. Her chest tightened, seeing how hard it was for him to open his eye. "Don't overexert yourself." She put her hand on his chest.

He let out a wet cough and she quickly rolled him on his side. He went on for a few minutes before his breathing calmed down again.

She rolled him back. His eyes, tired and lifeless, looked at her.

"Do you know what this is?" She showed him the symbol.

He looked at it and then coughed, but stopped himself from going into a fit. "Ancestor had it...judgement...be fair." Talking became harder for him and she stopped him from speaking anymore.

"Save your strength," she said.

He weakly tilted his head and closed his eyes.

She pushed his hair back. She would do anything in her power to see him alive and well, to see the suffering stop.

"Lady Tissis," the guard captain said.

She looked at him.

"We can't have you sick as well." The captain's voice was soft, knowing how hard it was for her to leave her husband like this.

She merely nodded and grit her teeth. She wanted to nurse him back to health but she had to keep the city going and weather through this.

She walked out of the room, taking some time to calm her emotions as she washed her hands thoroughly. As she did, she fought to control her mind. Seeing her husband like that cleared her mind more.

"If these Black Rags are doing good, make sure to monitor and help them. Make our statement clear: we are willing to help the people of Skalafell; we do not wish for violence. It will allow us to get some control over them in case they start trying to pull something," she told the guard captain.

"I will see to it," the guard captain said.

"As for the search for the people who attacked Keze, hold off for now. We need to deal with this crisis first before we break our forces apart." Tissis's anger had waned. They needed to survive first; then they could look at dealing with the issues.

The guard captain nodded.

"Go." She sent him on his way. She moved back to the office, feeling weaker than before but more stubborn as she walked with quick strides.

Night had fallen over the city, though she could see people with torches moving about in the darkness. The halls were lit up with magical devices and candles. She looked out of the office's windows as a flutter of light took her attention. She saw a pair of golden wings flap in the night sky before they disappeared from sight.

I'm starting to see things, I'm so tired. She laughed to herself and turned up the light in the room as she looked at the reports of food that had been compiled. "Just after winter when our stores are the lightest." She lifted up the papers to see a black letter.

It stuck out among the other reports and important letters.

She put down her report and turned the letter over in her hands. There was nothing to identify it. With a knife, she opened the letter.

It was of black paper, as well, with silver lettering on it.

"At this time, your husband is probably already at the point of dying. We have a cure, but are you worthy to receive it? If you tell anyone about this letter, you will never hear from us again. We contained the plague within this letter so you have already contracted it as well. Think wisely about your decision. Leave a light on in the northern tower and we will send further instructions about our cooperation. You don't have much time to wait. If not for your husband, than maybe your daughter. I have heard that it is terrible to lose a child."

She tore the piece of paper apart and threw it across the desk, letting out a frustrated yell and breathing heavily. She grabbed the letter and threw it in the fire. She ran to wash her hands; she gargled water and spit it out, hoping that it was all a lie.

She wiped her face but there was a conflicted expression on her face.

"Lady Tissis, there is a Commander Tysien from the camp to see you. She's been sent over to liaise," a guard said through the door.

"One second!" Tissis tried to compose herself as she looked in the mirror. She wanted to destroy the people who wrote that letter.

What if they really have a cure?

Her heart shook. She knew that her husband would never accept it, but seeing him in so much pain, thinking about Keze catching the plague...

She grabbed her mask and put it over her mouth and nose.

I'll have to keep her away from me to make sure that she won't catch it if I have it.

Her mind was a mess as she wondered just how the message had gotten on her desk. It was different from everything else and there were guards on her door, so someone must have snuck it in with the other messages and then got it past the guards somehow.

She shook her head and pulled herself together. It wasn't the time to be thinking about it.

"Let her in!" she yelled through the door. She walked back to her desk, seeing the fireplace give off a green flame as it burned through the paper.

Chapter: Under My Protection

Tysien entered the room and saw the lady of the city in command. "I am Commander Tysien. I was sent over to see if you have any needs."

"If you're not wearing a mask, it means that you intend to stay and you would have come earlier if you really cared about us, which means that something has changed and you're paying attention to it?" Tissis looked up from her desk, wearing her mask.

She was younger than Tysien but she had a presence and power on her side that made her only pale slightly compared to Jaclu.

Tysien made an awkward expression but didn't say anything.

"Well, it doesn't matter. You're now one of us—the damned of Skalafell—so I hope that your aid is not just empty promises or this city will be once the plague is done with us," Tissis said.

Tysien gritted her teeth, feeling like she was just tripping over her own feet. "I was wondering if there has been anything strange happening in Skalafell?"

There was a strange look in Tissis's eyes. Feeling something wrong, Tysien spoke up before Tissis could say anything. "There was a strange human who we believe might have entered the city."

"Oh, the rumored knight?" Tissis asked.

"Yes," Tysien said.

"He is going around the city, creating something of a legend, helping people out, I hear—helping to organize people, give them something to do. My people are going to help them out. That way, we can establish control in their ranks and make sure that their goals are aligned with the city's," Tissis said.

"That makes sense. These humans can be tricky. I also wish to see the city lord, if that is possible?"

"You are too bold!" Tissis slammed her hand against the desk. "You think because you treat us like rats that we're going to take it and allow you to walk all over us!"

Tysien gritted her teeth. It was her job to save and help these people but so far they had just stuffed these people in their own city and locked the doors from the outside, letting them fend for themselves. Tysien quickly pulled the bag off her hip. "I want to see if any of these work."

Tissis was breathing heavily, her mask moving in and out with every breath. She took out a bell and shook it.

A guard came through the door moments later.

"Have these taken to the healer and checked. Then have them administered to one of the willing sick to see if they are effective."

"Yes!" The guard took the items and then left.

"If one of them works, then we have supplies in the camp that we can give you. We don't like this situation any more than you but command thinks that this might be a ploy by the enemy to weaken our forces and that it was supposed to hit the camp and not the city. I can't do anything officially, but we all want to help you." Tysien thought of the people who the gnome and the elf had already rallied to their side to help the people in the city.

"It seems that the association of the Black Rags has already beaten you to it," Tissis said.

"Black Rags?"

"That is the group of people who have been organized by this knight and are helping the sick and injured," Tissis said.

"Oh?"

"Look, tensions are high and people are dying. I'm sorry I got angry with you. We need help and badly. I'm hoping that good will come from the Black Rags but while they mean well now, there's no knowing what they'll be like later on," Tissis said.

"They could take power into their own hands," Tysien said.

"Very much so," Tissis said.

There was a knock at the door.

"Come in!" Tissis yelled.

The door opened and a guard came in.

"Count Lemar is here. He's brought more healers and ingredients from his stores to help the city lord," the guard said.

Tissis's face softened. "Take him to see his brother right away and send my thanks. I will see him soon."

The guard bowed and headed out of the room.

"Count Lemar?"

"He's my husband's brother. My husband was adopted into the family and did well with their support but they have always been close," Tissis said.

Tysien pushed her lips into a smile and nodded.

"What aid can we get from the camp?" Tissis asked.

"Food, mainly. There are people gathering water filtration systems, masks, and soap as well," Tysien said.

***

"There is something strange going on here." Anthony sat on the wall of Skalafell, waving his feet in the air. Solomon appeared beside him and Bruce walked out on his arm, only showing his head.

"Shadow says that the guards are starting to help the Black Rags," Bruce said.

"Good. Make sure that they work well together, watch one another." Anthony reached into his boot, pulled out a map and looked at it.

Skalafell was shaped like part of a pie cut out, with two sides up against the water and then a third rounded-out wall that contained the city.

On his map, he was tracking all of the cases of the plague.

He had the Black Rags asking when people got affected so that Anthony was able to go back and track the progress of the plague.

He had made another map that looked at the original cases and where they worked or lived.

It created an interesting and strange picture.

"You would think that the nobles would be the last to be affected. From this, though, all of the people who served in the nobles' houses are the ones who must have spread it through the slums. The nobles are hiding from the people because they're the sickest, not because they have some kind of cure. Then there is a group going around, trying to incite looting and violence against the nobles, saying that they're the reason for this plague and that they're hoarding supplies. When taking a step back, it looks targeted. The next concentration is along the main streets.

"Solomon, give Aila a message. Tell her that what happened to the traders coming here—it might happen to others. I have a feeling that the Agents of Chaos are at work here." Anthony rolled the maps up and put them in his boot as part of the shadow beside him separated and rushed across the ground and out of the city.

"Now I need to rattle the tree and see what falls out." Anthony stood and looked over the city.

Solomon appeared and Bruce showed his head once again.

"There is a confrontation at the Mermaid square."

"Looks like I won't have to look far." Anthony jumped off the wall he was on. Dave's wings appeared as he glided down onto a roof.

He looked through a window and saw a badger kin boy staring at him with wide eyes. Anthony smiled to himself and gave the boy a thumbs-up. The boy smiled so wide it looked as if he were going to split his face as he held his bear and put his thumb up as well.

Anthony ran over the houses, gliding where he could.

It wasn't long until he reached the square, where there were two groups looking at one another, with Mai consoling a young man with a bloodied face.

"What is the meaning of this!" Mai stared at the group. They held sticks, gardening tools, and other implements, anger written on their faces.

Anthony watched from behind, ready to intervene if needed. *This is a good opportunity to observe and get information on this more violent group.*

A meerkat kin stood at the front of the group, wearing a red bandanna on his face. He gestured with his length of wood. "Look at you, pawns of the nobles! You're nothing in their eyes but you're doing their bidding. How do you have any pride!"

"We're helping out the city!"

"What has the city done for you! No one cares that you're trying to help. The nobles are probably rubbing their hands together because you're doing all the work of the guards!"

"We're—"

"Even working with them! Why don't you just say you like being their slaves!" the meerkat yelled over Mai. "Look at you all here. Is there even a knight behind you all? Where is he? Why isn't he helping out? He's probably some noble who got all dressed up and wanted to play hero!"

"He's not!" Mai yelled out.

"Hah! Look at you. You think you're some kind of leader because you say so? Don't you know how the people of Skalafell have been pushed down? The nobles are having parties in their homes while you're out here working! Slave."

"I'm not a slave," Mai yelled, balling his fists.

"Look—he has some fight in him!" The meerkat laughed, getting a few laughs from the group behind him.

"Either you help us in fighting the nobles and we take what is ours, or you are simply in our way! Don't you want to see the truth with your own eyes, to see the riches that they hoard away, the food that they throw away while we starve?"

The crowd behind the meerkat let out noises of agreement, raising their weapons and torches.

"What use will that be?"

"We will force them to help us! Force them to release their healing pills!" the meerkat yelled.

"Who knows if they even exist!" Mai yelled.

The meerkat scoffed at Mai. "What do you know, slave?" The meerkat stepped forward to look down at Mai. "We're real beasts, standing up for the honor of our people, seeking retribution, not slaves rooting around in the garbage, looking to get others' approval!"

The meerkat smiled, inviting Mai to punch him.

Anthony clapped his hands together. The sound of metal hitting metal crossed the square easily as they looked at the armored knight sitting on a roof, looking at the two parties.

Mai had a panicked look on his face. His anger dissipated and he touched his wrists.

"You did well, Mai. Now, my meerkat kin friend, what is your name?"

"I didn't realize it was a *human*!" the meerkat spat out, looking at all of the Black Rags with disgust.

The Black Rags looked at the human sitting on the roof in his armor in shock. They hadn't known that he was a human.

"Good, you've got eyes. Now I have a few questions for you lot." Anthony pushed off the building. Dave's wings grew from his back and people moved away from him, talking about his wings as he landed in front of the meerkat and his group.

"Who put you up to this?" Anthony asked.

"No one did!" one of the people in the crowd said.

"Filthy human! They're the enemy!"

"Even worse than nobles!" another yelled as the crowd moved forward.

The meerkat moved his head so that he looked down on Anthony, a look of power in his eyes. He sneered at him, letting the crowd rile themselves up.

Anthony let out a laugh. "Wow. You're just all pissed off, with nowhere to spend that energy in your lives. You ever thought about trying to do something else with your life, something that satisfies you a bit more?"

"You think you're better than us, human!" An angry older Badger-Kin waved his torch.

"How much did the nobles pay you to poison Skalafell?" the meerkat demanded. His question was like a match to the crowd's anger as they all started to move forward, murder in their eyes.

There were people in the Black Rags who had that same kind of anger as they looked at Mai and Anthony.

"They always taught me to be patient but I always told them that I wasn't that good at holding back," Anthony said.

"What do you have to say for your crimes?" another yelled.

"*My* crimes?" Anthony let out a low laugh that made people slow in their tracks as they felt something was wrong.

"What is this?"

"Is this mana?"

The power built around Anthony. The air seemed to crackle with energy as they all looked at him. The meerkat had an uneasy look on his face as he unconsciously stepped back half a step.

"Stop there!" A yell came from a side street. A woman stood atop of her mount, with a halberd at her side.

Anthony's eyes thinned. He felt a flare of anger from his arm. *"Bruce?"*

"Seems that this young one has no respect. Will you give me the power to materialize?"

Anthony took a moment. *"You've got it,"* Anthony said.

Bruce let out a grunt in thanks as all of the beast kin around Anthony paused.

"Is this bloodline pressure?"

"Isn't he a human though?"

Both groups were confused at the pressure that was coming off Anthony as the mana in the area continued to gather around Anthony.

"Human tricks!" the meerkat yelled out, pointing at Anthony. "He wants to kill us all with the plague or enslave us!"

"Shut! Up!" Anthony landed two crisp slaps on the meerkat's face. "There are people's lives on the line and you want to incite violence! You wish to cause issues in a city that is under my protection!" Anthony's voice grew deeper, gaining greater power. The bloodlines within the beast kin boiled as they were forced to kneel.

"You test my patience!"

Bruce materialized above Anthony and looked over those there. Their foreheads slammed into the ground.

Only Tysien was able to stop herself. Her mount was lowered in supplication but she was keeping her head up, looking at the familiar. "Clan spirit." The words escaped her mouth and her face paled.

"May I deal with this one?" the clan spirit asked Anthony. He was like an emperor standing tall above all others.

"She's your offspring," Anthony said.

"She is nothing but a girl, a hypocrite and a shame to my bloodline," Bruce said. "You accused my friend of crimes he did not commit, were prejudiced toward him because of his race. You came into the city only after he entered to watch him. Instead of trying to stop the fighting here, you watched; we intervened and then you wanted him to get hurt, wanted to see your beliefs fulfilled. What kind of ignorant child are you? Are you so vindictive that you want others to suffer for no other reason but to prove your own misguided beliefs!" Bruce dropped to the ground and grew in size so he was the size of a small house as he looked down at Tysien.

She dropped forward in supplication, gritting her teeth.

Bruce turned into a beast kin. As he reached out, Tysien flew forward and into his hand. He bent her over his knee.

A ringing smack sounded out and Tysien grunted, holding back tears.

"Children will be treated as children!" Bruce barked as he smacked her backside again. In front of him, she was no stronger than a toddler.

"You are a member of the legion, a member of my clan, and instead of helping those in need, restoring the balance, you were willing to allow others slide into chaos!" Two more smacks rang out as the others shook in fear.

A total of five smacks landed on Tysien's backside. She forced tears back, blood on her lips and the injustice clear in her eyes.

Bruce shook his head. "I can see it in your eyes. Look at me, girl."

Tysien forced her head up and looked into Bruce's eyes—eyes that had seen the pass of centuries, the rises and the falls of Dena and the beast people. A progenitor of the bull clan.

She unconsciously relaxed looking into them, seeing the care and feeling ashamed seeing the frustration.

"Anthony over there has his own worries to deal with. We work together to deal with those issues," Bruce said in a soft voice that was filled with a timeless quality.

"You erred. As much as you're trying to put that blame on Anthony, what has he done to you? Against you? He has started to build support for this city, looked to help people who have been looked down on by one another and others for the clan that they come from." Bruce raised his voice so that others could hear him and feel the anger within. "That are now looking down on others with their small-minded thoughts! That instead of banding together and seeing one another as people of Dena, they are looking to be divisive and create a rift between groups of Skalafell. Build, help, and work hard."

Bruce gave her one more look as he stood up from kneeling.

"Do you know why the nobles are hiding in their homes? It's because they are dying. Their entire families are dying within those compounds. None of the medical supplies are working. They're too weak to leave their homes. But, here you are, pissed off with life, pissed off that you feel like you can't do anything; you feel like you can't go anywhere." Bruce shook his head. "Nothing is instantaneous. It takes time—it takes hard work to get what you want. You feel like you're spinning your wheels—that is no one's fault but yours. It is your life. You need to take control of it, instead of blaming others for the fact it isn't working out. You want to piss people off because of the inner joy it gives you? That sadistic little part of joy you get in the back of your head? That is the true poison, the poison that will corrode you from the inside. We don't have long in this world—do you want to spend it being the asshole who started a fight in the middle of a plague, or the person who brought food and water to those who couldn't move from bed?"

Bruce let out a tired sigh and looked at Anthony. "Charge them. Hopefully they'll learn." He turned into a green light and entered Anthony's arm.

A purple hammer appeared in Anthony's hand and the Guardian emblem lit up. He dropped the meerkat. He swung his hammer and a crisp sound rang out through the square. The mana that had gathered formed into a table and desk; six more seats appeared as judges sat in their own seats.

There was a pig kin judge this time. He crossed his hands in front of him, glowering at the men and women in front of him.

"Neutral mindset," Anthony said.

"I will listen to their crimes. For daring to hurt their kin and clan, I will not be kind," the beast kin said.

The other judges refrained from speaking, silently acknowledging his authority.

"Do you want to seat this judgement?" Anthony asked.

The pig kin stood and cupped his hands. "This city is under your protection, Guardian, and I thank you for your offer. I will not refuse, but for sentencing I will need all of your help."

The pig kin looked to all of the judges, who nodded and smiled.

"Aren't we people of Dena?" the dwarven judge asked. The hob judge let out a hooting laugh of agreement.

Anthony held out the hammer and it flowed out into the pig kin judge's hands. He seemed to come into focus more.

"I bring this court into session!" His voice was low but it contained a deep power. The beast kin shivered, looking at the man as he tapped his gavel.

"For the crimes of raising a public disturbance, for wishing to gather a mob in a time of chaos, and incite violence and suffering among the population, how do you plead?" he asked.

"Guilty!" There were a smatterings of "innocents" from the crowd.

"We will start with the first defendant," the pig kin man said, his voice like rolling thunder on the horizon. His expression darkened.

Everyone shivered under his gaze, as if seeing their own parents' disappointment and disgust.

***

Tysien was bound by her bloodline. She knew that it was a clan spirit that had publicly humiliated her. She was burning with anger at Anthony for putting her in this situation.

She couldn't think of how she was waiting for him to get involved in the situation, to become part of the issue so that she would have a way to lock him up so that he would never be able to leave. So he couldn't lie and deceive others. Now she saw him sitting there at his table, one of six other judges as they reviewed case after case.

They were listening to the defendants' reasonings; they were entranced after the questions were asked, leaving them no way to lie to the judges.

She had never seen anything like it as people's crimes were revealed in front of everyone. Sentencing was swift and quick, with the judges operating like a machine to work through the cases and make sure that everyone had a fair trial.

What is going on with me?

She shivered, not sure just where her mind was going. The more she watched, the less her mind could defend her, as she saw Anthony working, not leading the judges but one of them, listening to them and allowing the pig kin judge to lead them all.

Her thoughts turned inward and she shifted around awkwardly, thinking of what she had done to someone else, of how nasty she had been, and the way that she had acted. She felt shame, looked for ways to make it not that bad, to prove to herself that she wasn't that bad.

As she couldn't, she started to feel worse, spiraling.

Now the dam had broken and she had started to think in a new vein, she no longer watched the trials. She started to think when and where she had gone wrong, why she thought the way that she did.

She wanted nothing more than to dig a hole and hide in it.

***

"I would like to call a recess." Anthony looked to the other judges.

They looked at one another and agreed.

"A five-minute recess." The pig kin's gavel tapped and the tables wrapped up into a circle. A purple barrier blocked one from seeing what was happening inside.

Anthony looked at the judges. "I feel like this group and others are brought about by Agents of Chaos. We went through a group of them who were trying to transform people in a blood ritual outside of the city. When looking at the area, it seems that those affected are in certain high-traffic areas. The most affected are the nobles and there is someone targeting them when they can't defend themselves." Anthony left his words hanging there.

The judges all had dark expressions.

"It does seem that there is someone with a different agenda here," the elemental judge said.

"I don't feel like the majority of them know what is happening—they were just stirred up," the elven judge said.

"We'll get to the bottom of it," the pig kin assured them.

They finished their recess and looked back at the accused.

Many of them had been forced into community service for their crimes of trying to harm others when they needed their help more than ever.

People were arguing and complaining, but all of the Black Rags stood there, glaring at those guilty of trying to carry out violence just because they thought that they could.

More people had gathered. With the group of rioters' crimes being examined and read out, the older generation were tutting and displeased, while the younger generation had a fire in their eyes. They were all supposed to be citizens of Skalafell, working together but instead they had been shown the disappointing truth of some of their fellow citizens.

"Next defendant!" the pig kin said.

A duck kin stepped out, with broken feathers and other scratches and blemishes. Even though he was from one of the smaller and weaker races, he was much larger than other duck kin.

"Tungur!" a honking duck voice called out over the square as Tungur seemed to be trying to make himself smaller.

An older-looking duck stood there with a cane. She glared at the younger duck kin. Beside her, there was a younger duck kin man with a smaller build than Tungur but similar features and his arms crossed.

Grandmother and father—well, it's his fault for being an ass, Anthony thought. There was a hierarchy in all of the clans. Going against those who were older was dishonorable on everyone.

"You have pled guilty for trying to disrupt the operation of the city and to try to incite violence with your fellow citizens. Do you understand these accusations?" the pig kin said.

There was a deep honking noise from the boy's father. His grandmother stood there with her hands resting on her cane.

Tungur stared at the ground. "I understand, Mister."

"Were you coerced into this action by any other party?"

"I wasn't, sir," Tungur answered to the ground.

"You were looking to incite violence from the beginning or did someone invite you to start a riot?" the head judge asked.

Tungur looked up, his eyes in a daze. "I was asked if I wanted to join and my friend Kleo asked me multiple times, told me about the nobles looking down on us and I couldn't help but want to get back at them. My parents and grandmother forbade me from doing anything and wanted me to join the Black Rags to help our neighbors, but Kleo said that they were just the slaves of the nobles. I wanted to show my family that I could affect change, to show my strength and be recognized more. Treated like an adult." Tungur's eyes cleared. He looked down in shame, sending a glance at his family.

"How do you think that has gone? Do you feel like more of an adult now?" the pig kin judge asked, his voice damning.

Tungur shuffled his feet and didn't answer. As he wasn't under compulsion and wasn't part of the case, he wasn't forced to answer truthfully.

"Judges, I believe that he will serve with the Black Rags for the remaining time. He will look after supplies, food, and water for those who are unable to get it themselves."

The others nodded their agreement.

He used his gavel and then manacles appeared around Tungur's wrists as he shifted the wings that lay down along his sides.

"I'll pass him to you now." The pig kin looked at the father and grandmother.

"Clan spirit." The grandmother's stormy expression cleared as she curtsied and the father tucked his wings back and bowed.

The pig kin clan spirit nodded as Tungur waddled away from the defendant's podium.

"Kleo, are you here?"

A mole kin stepped forward.

"Defendant Kleo, it is good to see you. You have pled guilty..."

The court continued on, quickly charging people, handing out punishments, and keeping things going. Mai, Jun, and Ubi had showed up. The guilty parties went over there, filled with shame, only to see that Ubi, Jun, and Mai all had purple chains on their wrists as well.

They felt a little better, until they saw the stormy expressions on the trio's faces.

Running the Black Rags for only a few days, they had learned just how bad things were in Skalafell.

The more they saw, the angrier they were with themselves for threatening the little miss Keze. They only slept when they needed to, and Anthony had a feeling that they would have the guilty "volunteers" quickly following in their footsteps, even if they didn't want to.

They were sent off across the city as Ubi, Jun, and Mai's presence also made those who were watching and were part of the Black Rags quickly run off and see to their duties. Others who had heard about the group started to learn more about them as people went to the marked walls, adding information or carrying out tasks that were listed.

A gloominess had covered Skalafell. Few people gathered in public places, but the event had brought the people together since the plague had first showed up. People even offered their own information to help the Black Rags and reduce the load on them.

Anthony discreetly paid attention to the head judge's probing questions, chasing the people who had influenced others to join the rioting group, exposing their leadership as the community watched on with displeased looks. *This wasn't spontaneous; someone was organizing it all.*

People in the crowd started to catch on as well as more leaders were brought forward and exposed, getting worse sentences than others who had just been part of the issues instead of starting them.

It wasn't long until they got to the meerkat kin that had been leading the group.

"Mister Rody Barrett, by all accounts, you are the de facto leader of this little band. Why did you become their leader?"

"I would get paid and was told that my family would be cared for. The nobles have always looked down on us. This way, I would be able to get power with the people. I could make money as well and my family's health would be secured," the meerkat kin said.

"Who gave you this offer?"

"I do not know their name," Rody said.

"Do you know where we can find them?"

"They contacted me."

"Do you have any information about them?"

"They knew about the plague, said that if I was able to distract the nobles then they would be able to steal from the nobles and secure a cure for the plague and share it with me and my family."

The others who had been part of the group now all looked at Rody with accusation in their eyes. They knew that they would be going up against the nobles in the city, but he was using them as a cover so that someone else could steal a cure for his family.

"Did he ever give you evidence to show that the nobles had some cure?" the pig kin asked.

"No. They promised me, though," Rody said.

"Oh, a promise from someone you don't know, don't know how to contact?" the pig kin asked. "Did they give you anything that made you think that they would follow through?"

"They helped me find the people who were annoyed with the nobles and gather them. They told me about secrets that the nobles have that no normal person would know and they paid me money," Rody said.

"How much money?"

"Forty gold coins, with a promise of a share of what they looted, which could be in the hundreds of gold. If we sold off the cures, then it would be more."

"Did they just plan to steal from one noble?"

"No, they wanted to steal from a number of them," Rody said.

"Which nobles?"

"The Haskas, Vrykn, Lemar, and Mesen families were their major targets."

"Was there anything odd about them? Did you find there was an odd smell in the air or that your bloodline felt weaker after you met with them?"

"Yes," Rody said.

The judge's eyes focused on Rody before a few of them glanced at one another.

Anthony leaned forward, resting his head on his hand while he tapped on the table with his finger. *Pretty much confirms that the person who was talking to him had the power of chaos inside their body, which caused his bloodline to reject it and went a little haywire.* His jawbone opened; he looked like a laughing skeleton inside his helmet. His glowing eyes turned colder. *Too bad for them I was in the area. For them to be this powerful to affect the running of a city and introduce a plague right next to a camp of legionnaires... There aren't any gates open to their lands yet. I need to get stronger so that I can deal with more of these problems and remove the Agents of Chaos from Dena.*

The trial continued.

"You used the people of Skalafell for your own means, not caring about the lives of others in the process. You will serve as a member of the Black Rags for the remainder of the plague. Once the plague is cured, then for seven years you will not hold more than ten silver at one time and must donate it or use it to buy supplies or items for those who are in need. You will carry out tasks to assist your community at least three times a week. You will take up meditation and meditate on what you have done once a day."

Rody was pale as he stood there, no more words coming out as his crimes were revealed to all. He shook in fear as the head judge struck his gavel.

Those who were part of the riot sent Rody dirty looks while their faces burned in shame as they and the others of their community and city heard of how they were being led around by someone who just wanted to lash out at the nobles because he was on a power trip and he was promised a cure that he wasn't willing to pass onto anyone else.

The remaining trials went quickly. A few were found to have hidden crimes and were charged accordingly.

Some were found to actually be innocent but they were in the minority.

The pig kin struck the gavel as they all stood up.

"Judgement has been passed."

The pig kin turned to Anthony and cupped his fists. "It has been a pleasure serving with you, Guardian. Even your legends have made it to our plane. Good luck and stay safe."

Anthony returned the gesture. "Thank you for your help."

The judges and the courtroom disappeared and Anthony was left standing there.

Those in the square looked at him in a different manner.

"Skalafell will make it through this plague. We will need to work together," Anthony said.

Anthony saw the looks in their eyes. There was fear and respect and also confusion. They had been taught to hate humans all of this time, but instead of attacking them and being the sort of demon that most humans were, Anthony helped them freely. He didn't suffer fools and a clan spirit had actually come under his command, becoming his familiar.

"I'll be watching." With that, he ran and jumped, grabbing Tysien by the armor. Dave's wings appeared on his back and he cleared the square, leaving it in just a few wing beats.

He found a rooftop and dropped her on it as he drifted to the ground. Now, seeing the woman, he could feel his anger welling up as he looked over the city.

"Some of my best friends were from the legion. Are they like you? I will not let their history or their legion become tainted." Anthony looked back at Tysien.

She had a defiant look on her face but it crumbled under his gaze. "You wouldn't."

"I once brought an entire dwarven mountain to judgement. Don't test me, girl," Anthony said.

"I'm not a girl!"

"Oh, really? I've seen nothing to convince me otherwise."

"I'm probably older than you! Have you ever been in a battle? You don't even have any scratches on your armor!"

"I am a spritely one hundred and thirteen years old. Do you want to compare ages again?" Anthony asked dryly.

"What?" Tysien choked on her words. "But humans don't live for that long."

"Weak ones won't," Anthony said.

"Who are you?"

"Guardian Anthony. Now, answer the question. Will I need to clear the legions? Have they become corrupted?"

"I—" Tysien was at a loss for words.

Anthony sighed. His anger fell away, replaced with sadness instead. He looked over at the city. It seemed darker now.

"Things changed while I was gone," he said to himself. He saw memories of walking up to buildings with the Guardian's crest. On the outside, everything was orderly and clean but in the back, there would be people wearing armor and gear of all kinds, laughing and joking, competing with one another, from all of the races. Sharing a drink or some food as they caught up or got to know one another.

Seeing them all was like going home.

They fought hard and played harder, placing their lives in one another's hands as they challenged the forces of chaos together, roamed the front lines and charged toward the gates, leading the united armies of Dena.

Now he looked at a city that was broken.

Their trust in one another is no longer there, but with time I'll be able to pull them back, be able to bring them together once again. I need to get back my power and my memories. I can only use Guardian's Judgement because it pulls from the ambient mana and channels it through the formations that are on my armor. For calling out my familiars, I was nearly drained with Bruce taking form for that long. My power is recovering but it is taking too long. I still haven't been able to wake up Wendy and Penelope.

"There is a power in this city, a power of chaos, agents that come from another world and that want to consume ours to increase their power and numbers. They consume all other forms of power to grow. I believe that they are at work here. They are using this situation to make people stop trusting one another, increase tensions. Their aim is to make us fight in our backlines and attack one another so that when they come across through their gates, then they just clean up the divided pieces. It is going to be our task to search them out and find out just what plague they have created. You will now coordinate supplies, the forces of the city, and the Black Rags to help the people within the city while I will search out these Agents of Chaos and their minions," Anthony said.

"Okay." Tysien looked at the city, not wanting to look at Anthony.

Chapter: Chaos Emerges

"Move it! Come on!" Aila yelled as people piled up their foodstuffs along the wall on pallets.

"This load is done." The quartermaster wore a mask, muffling his voice.

"Move to the second loading area!" she yelled to the carriage drivers.

They moved on toward and down the wall.

The quartermaster and his people moved back from the pallets that were attached to ropes that went up the wall to arms that hung over the side of Skalafell's battlements. They moved to a sanitary station, washing their hands thoroughly under the watchful eyes of healers and medics.

Aila blew a whistle.

There were a few moments before there was movement on the walls.

People manned the different arms and worked together to pull up the pallets, the much-needed food, masks, soap, and water filtration systems being raised up.

They reached the top of the wall and then turned, disappearing over it.

Aila looked at the next loading area, where another team was unloading the items from the traders' carriages, then loading them onto waiting pallets.

That's the first batch of supplies. I hope that there is some kind of cure.

She looked at the train of carriages. Boats were unloading what they could spare on the other side of the river, passing it down to the boats that then shipped it to the shore, where they were piled onto carriages that would carry them off over one of the main bridges and to Skalafell.

Beast kin and traders from the isles and Selenus were working together to try to help out the people of Skalafell, letting them know that they weren't alone.

There were traders who grumbled and complained, but most traded here all the time; they had friends inside the city as well.

***

Tissis looked at her husband. He was weaker than he had ever been.

She wanted to go and let him rest his head on her lap as she cared for him. Instead, she watched from the side, wearing her own mask, watching the man she loved waste away.

Her thoughts drifted back to that letter as she took one last look at him and then left the room. Since she had gotten the letter, she hadn't seen Keze. For fear that what it said was true, she hadn't taken her mask off either.

She went to her office, sitting down as she looked at the mounting reports. *Thankfully the Black Rags are actually what they seem to be—just a group of people trying to help out one another. Though they don't know that there is nothing that they can do for those affected.*

She closed her eyes. A few tears fell out of her eyes and she started to cry.

"What did we do to deserve this?" she asked pitifully. Her pain turned to anger as she yelled and threw the books and reports on her desk to the side, tossing things all over the place before she felt the fight go out of her as she fell back into her seat, tired and defeated.

She started coughing from her exertion. There was a knock at the door.

"Everything okay, my lady?" the guard asked.

"Fi-ne," she fought through the coughing.

"Understood!" the guard said.

She let out the coughing, taking a few minutes before she calmed down.

She was breathing heavy as she remembered the look in the healer's eyes as he confirmed that none of the concoctions had helped to clear the plague that was killing her husband from the inside.

She was looking down when she noticed something on her arm. She rolled up her sleeve a bit and her hands started to shake. Faint red dots had appeared on her skin. Fear gripped her, her entire body going cold.

What will happen to Keze if we both die?

Shock rolled through her system as she looked at the fireplace. She wanted to order her guards forth and destroy whoever had sent that letter—whoever had given her and her husband the plague.

She wanted to tear them apart but they were the only people who could possibly help her and her family.

I'll find a cure. I'll find some way to reverse this and then I'll hunt them down and destroy them! Her claws were out, digging into the armrests of her chair.

In her agitation, she started to cough once more, unable to stop it. Her whole body convulsed.

She finally stopped, her body shaking and weak from the effort.

She rubbed her face and fur came away with her hand.

Can I wait?

That thought made her feel so helpless and small. She knew the right thing to do, but did the right thing outweigh what she wanted to do because of her family?

She debated as night fell.

Inside, she was a mess. But she gathered her strength, grabbing a candle and hiding it in a pocket with a fire starter.

She exited her office and walked to the northern wing, her guards following her.

"I'm just going to get some fresh air in the tower," she said to them both.

"I'll check it to make sure that it is clear," one said.

She nodded as they quickly went up the spiral stairs. It took them a few minutes before they returned.

"All clear, my lady," he said.

She smiled to him and made sure not to get too close as she headed up the stairs. Her mind was resolute, but it didn't stop the fears or the other thoughts from intruding as she walked step by step, feeling as if she were crossing some unknown barrier that went against everything that she believed in.

Reaching the top, she stood there, looking over Skalafell. People were working on the walls, bringing in supplies that were distributed by the Black Rags. *It feels like I'm betraying them, but I have to do this for the city, for Keze. Once we have the cure, then we can make sure that the people who made this plague suffer.* A part of her knew that she was lying to herself but she didn't want to admit that.

She took out the candle and put it into a candle holder. She took a deep breath of the cold air as she took out her fire starter, using it on the candle.

The candle took and she stared at it for a few minutes. She looked away in shame and then descended the stairs, not looking back.

She reached the bottom of the stairs. It felt as if she were lying to everyone as she walked back to her office and slumped down in her chair. She looked at the flames in the fireplace. Even as they burned, she didn't feel any of their warmth.

***

Tissis didn't know when she finally got up from her office and went to the room that was attached to it. She didn't care to remove her dress as she lay down, looking at the moonlight through her curtains.

Even with all of her fears and emotions, it wasn't enough to keep her from sleep.

Nightmares plagued her mind before her eyes suddenly snapped open, sensing that there was something wrong. She jumped up as she realized that there was now a new shadow in the room. Someone was sitting in a chair next to the window, looking at her.

"It seems that you've come to a decision, your ladyship. We saw the candle in the tower." It was a man's voice but it held a hint of ridicule.

"How did you get in here?" she demanded, looking around, debating calling her guards.

"Those secret entrances, catacombs and such, they really are incredibly complicated, but if you have the time and patience, or a *guide,* then they're not so hard to move through."

She could feel the man's smile as a shiver ran up her spine. There were a number of hidden escape routes in the lord's manor, not only in the lord's office but in different private quarters of the lord's family.

There's a secret entrance in Keze's room! She started to ball her fists as the man talked.

"There's no need to get angry, Miss Tissis. I'm merely here as a messenger with an offer."

"Do you have a cure?" Tissis hissed.

"Of course we do. Do you think that I would be this healthy otherwise?" The man laughed. "Or so close to one of the people with the plague? Though we just need you to do something for us before we can give you it."

"What?" Tissis had already stepped on the path; she needed to know where it would lead.

"You see, it looks like everything has calmed down here a bit. I like more *excitement,* more anger, distrust—general *chaos.*"

A wave of nausea passed over her, making her feel weak and causing her blood to tremble. *Is this some kind of bloodline-based attack?* She steadied herself and studied her body but there was nothing wrong with her on a physical level.

"Please, take a seat." The man relaxed, as if he knew that nothing would happen to him.

Tissis moved to the couch opposite, her eyes never leaving the man. "What do you want?" she asked through gritted teeth.

"Oh, right to the point. I do like it." The man smiled. "This Black Rags thing has been annoying me and my people for some time. I want you to break them apart. You know, kill a few of their members, scatter the rest." The man shrugged, leaving the rest to her.

"If I was to do that, then the city would turn on me."

"Oh, well, they do say that health is the most important thing and I trust that the other nobles won't be around to help you. Seems that the *plague* affected them more than any other group."

"How do I know that you'll uphold your end of the bargain?"

"You don't," the man said with a wicked grin. "Isn't that *exciting*!"

He laughed at her warping expression.

"Don't worry, someone has given your daughter the cure tonight so she won't be affected by it, but your husband will need to get the cure soon if he wants to survive." The man waved his hand as a spell he'd had prepared shot out and hit Tissis.

She didn't have time to yell out as the magical power drained her and caused her to collapse, falling into a slumber. She woke some time later, sitting on the couch. There was no sign of the man.

Tissis gritted her teeth, taking a few moments and closing her eyes to calm herself. All she could see behind her closed eyes was her husband's face as he grew weaker each day.

She moved to the adjacent office, lighting a lamp there, and she pulled out a piece of paper.

I have to do this, for my family.

She took out a brush and started to write down new orders for her guards. She felt sick to her stomach as she wrote out the orders. She couldn't think what might come from her orders being carried out.

How many families will be affected? How many will be hurt?

***

Anthony roamed the roofs and the streets. Based on the information that Rody had given him, he was looking in the places that the meerkat kin had met up with the Agents of Chaos. The different places didn't have any traces of chaotic energy left to them. The places where the money had been dropped off were similarly blank.

He marked out the positions of the meeting places and drop points. All of them were randomly placed, giving no true pattern.

Anthony moved across the city, with Solomon appearing from time to time. Based on his reports, Anthony would rush across the city, using his healing ability to only relieve the symptoms of the cursed plague.

It was as if he stood before a fire: he could put out the flames, but he couldn't put out the embers, no matter what. If he just turned away, then that ember would re-ignite and there was that much less wood to burn.

He wasn't saving them, just prolonging their remaining time.

Solomon appeared next to Anthony as Bruce's head appeared.

"He says that there is something strange happening at the castle."

Anthony looked over at the castle that stood above the city. *"Anything more specific? If I break in there, then we might run into some trouble."*

"He says that some of his shadows can feel a disturbance, says that it is like chaotic power," Bruce said.

"Okay, track it, Solomon, and guide me to it. I'll stay outside until we can confirm it," Anthony said.

***

Count Lemar looked to his side as his aide returned.

"Where did you go?" Lemar hissed.

"You don't really expect me to answer that, do you, Count Lemar?" the aide said.

"Just make sure to keep your side of the deal."

"Don't worry, you'll soon become the city lord of Skalafell and have Tissis in your arms while your adopted brother will have a long and painful death," the "aide" said.

Lemar's eyes flashed in anger and his hands bawled into fists. "He was nothing but an adopted runt, but he thought that he could stand on my head, taking the woman I liked from me, taking the position of city lord. I'm just correcting the balance, returning things to the way that they should be."

"Yes, my city lord," the aide said.

Lemar didn't see the playful smile on the aide's face.

They left the room that they were staying in.

"Did you hear, there were a group of people trying to start a riot. Then there was this *human* who walked between them and the Black Rags. He used some kind of magic that brought down a clan spirit and all of these judges. They went through the rioters, charged them all with crimes and gave them sentences. It looks like they weren't rioting for the good of the people, but because they were pissed off and wanted to do something that would impact others and make them feel good in their own way. There is a plague going on and they want to try to use it to hurt others," one servant said as the other shook their head.

"They were able to summon judges?"

Count Lemar looked back to see that his aide was talking to the servants.

"Yes sir," one of the servants said. Both of them bobbed their heads nervously, being caught out for gossiping instead of working.

"Was the courtroom purple?"

"I'm not sure, sir."

"Did someone talk about Guardians, or Guardian's Judgement?"

"That sounds familiar. I think so, but I'm not sure," the other said.

"I thought that someone was just trying to use old symbols from the past. I didn't think that there might be someone related to the Guardians here. I thought we were able to get rid of them all. If there are still any left, I don't know why they would be advertising their presence so loudly."

Lemar looked at his aide, who was stuck in thought.

Guardians? Judgement? Just who are these people to make him look confused? He's always seemed like he knows everyone's moves.

Chapter: Leader Of The Black Rags

"Are you sure of this, Lady Tissis?" the guard captain asked as he read the orders she had passed him.

"Have you forgotten your oath?" Tissis said, her eyes cold and her voice dangerous.

"No." It seemed as though the guard captain wanted to say more but saluted instead.

There was a knock at the door.

"What is it?" Tissis snapped.

"The leader of the Black Scarves is here!" someone yelled through the door.

"What is he doing here?" The guard captain frowned.

Tissis paled. *Does he know? How could he know? They say that he is powerful and he was able to stop a riot in its tracks. Is he coming here to get more help, to pressure me? Does he know what is going on?*

Tissis needed a few seconds to get herself under control. "Send him in." Tissis then looked at the guard captain. "Make sure that you have people ready."

"Yes, my lady." The guard captain quickly left.

Tissis cleaned up her office as she waited. It wasn't long until the leader of the Black Rags walked into the office.

He is a human indeed, though I can't see through his armor.

"Lady Tissis," the man said in greeting as two guards came into the room with him.

***

Chaos, Anthony thought. Everything was telling him that there had been an Agent of Chaos or a person converted with the power of chaos in this room just a few hours ago.

Anthony used his Eyes of Truth to look at Tissis.

"You must be the leader of the Black Rags, Anthony?" Lady Tissis looked at him from the other side of her desk.

"I thought that someone should help out with the chaos around here." Anthony watched her closely. *She seems a bit awkward, but the word chaos didn't seem to affect her.*

"Many people have told me that they feel a fluctuation in their bloodlines, as if someone is cutting them off from their ancestors."

Bingo, she's come into contact with one. Anthony could read her emotions as if they were an open book.

Anthony looked up at the painting that was behind the office desk. "The battle of Xindez," Anthony said, picking out the different terrain features. His eyes noticed the Guardian emblem at the top of the painting.

"You know of it?" Tissis asked.

"You could say that." Anthony took a moment, seeing the painting come to life in his mind, the fierce fighting as the forces of Dena collided with the chaos vanguard. It was one of the first battles between the people of Dena. They hadn't been fully united; the humans and the beast kin were fighting different waves of chaos that flooded through their gates.

"So now, tell me about when you came in contact with someone affected by chaos." Anthony's hand rested on his swords and the two guards in the room tensed up.

Tissis looked at Anthony.

"They should have been here only a few hours ago. Did you make a deal with them?"

Tissis opened and closed her mouth. Her features started to twist as shadows shot out from Anthony's feet. Solomon wrapped around the guards' and Tissis's feet and mouths.

"Do not test me, little lady." Anthony's voice transformed, sounding like a demon that had clawed his way out of hell. "Did you make a deal with someone just hours ago? It would have been in your room?

He entered and left through a secret passage in this room." Anthony walked up to the desk, his hand on his sword.

"It looks like you did." Anthony could read her expression clearly. "What was your deal?" Anthony used a spell. He was drained from having powered such a large Guardian's Judgement. He felt as though he were scraping the bottom of the barrel as his spell hit Tissis. Her eyes went glossy and Solomon moved away.

"I made a deal with him to heal me and my husband. In exchange, I would need to break the Black Rags apart."

Solomon wrapped around her mouth; the guards looked at her in shock and her eyes cleared and widened in alarm.

"Okay, have you had any other dealings with them?" Anthony watched her and nodded. "That would be a no. Have you done anything to carry out their actions?" He let out a sigh at her expression.

"Do you know anything about them that would allow me to identify them?" Her expression changed again. "Okay, so I'll need to move fast if I want to follow his trail." Anthony moved to her desk and rooted around in it quickly. Solomon destroyed his shadows across the city so Anthony could use more of them to search the drawers. Anthony pulled out a guard badge and then wrote a letter, sealing it with the Skalafell lord's seal. "That should help."

Anthony put the crest on his armor and then moved to the two guards in just a few steps.

With two hits, their eyes rolled back and they fell on the floor.

Anthony took them into the bedroom, using the sheets to tie them up.

"When I return, you'll undergo judgement," Anthony said.

Tissis's eyes were wide as Anthony hit her, knocking her out. He took her into the bedroom and tied her up.

He followed the stain of chaos and went to a bookshelf. He pushed the bottom to the side and crawled through the hidden passage there.

He closed the hidden entrance behind him and rushed forward. The chase was on!

Anthony slammed through a hidden door, coming out into another room in a spray of wood.

"Ah, they were just here!" Anthony yelled as he ran forward, hitting the doors out of the room. Something feral had woken up in him. The power of his familiars was stronger than ever, more powerful than adrenaline. People jumped out of the way of the mad knight running through the halls.

He ran past two servants, eyeing them because they had come into direct contact with a chaotic being. They both screamed and jumped.

"Official business!" Anthony yelled, holding out his badge as he kept on running through the halls. He saw a large beast kin marching down the hall, a number of guards with him.

Anthony started to laugh as the group turned around to look at the knight closing in with them.

The guards started to move to block his path.

"Chaos! I've come for you!" Anthony's eyes glowed with a fierce light under his helmet. His face formed a twisted smile.

"Guardian!" One of the men with the count turned and ran.

"What are you doing!" the count hissed.

Anthony moved forward. A blade came for his head. He shot past the attacker in a burst of golden speed. His body glowed green as he grabbed their arm, tossing them into a wall. Then he grabbed a blade coming through the air, snapping it in half as he kicked the guard into another behind them.

He arrived in front of the count, who was powering up. Two quick smacks disoriented the beast kin. Anthony picked him up by the torso and slammed him into a wall where there was an arrangement of swords.

A golden head appeared over Anthony's shoulder, breathing on the blades. A black shadow emerged from the wall. A demon mask looked at the beast kin as its shadow tendrils pushed the blades down around the count, so that he had no room to move, the sword acting as a prison.

"I'll talk to you later."

Anthony's armor glowed green while his joints leaked a black miasma and golden wings appeared on his back.

He looked where the chaos-touched being was running and then looked toward a window.

Anthony took a run and leaped out of the window. The rough glass window shattered around him as Dave's wings unfurled. The early morning sun spread over Skalafell as a demon took to the skies.

Anthony banked around, picking up speed. He took in a deep breath, banking wide and then toward the building.

His wings collapsed as he darkened the window. His helmet lit up with his blue eyes as he saw the Agent of Chaos who had just reached the top of the stairs.

A swirl of gold, green and black appeared in Anthony's eyes as he drew on the power of his familiars.

The Agent of Chaos' hood had come back, revealing his elven features and the look of panic on his face as he saw Anthony in front of him.

Anthony went through another window as the Agent of Chaos let out a yell that contorted into a roar; his body shimmered, shook, started and stopped—elvish one moment and chaotic beast the other, made from contorted and alternating colors. It stood six foot tall, had black feet and claws, with a body that looked like glass, allowing one to see the twisted power inside its body.

"Guardian!" the elf yelled out before he broke his restraints, shuddering between forms and becoming a chaotic beast.

Anthony crashed through the window as the chaotic creature fired off a pillar of chaos energy. A mana shield appeared around Anthony, but he was like a rock in front of a hose. The power was breaking around him, as he forced his way upstream.

"Judgement comes." Anthony drew his sword and pushed it forward.

A purple energy shot forward into the chaos. The beam disappeared, with silence returning in an almost painful fashion. Anthony gritted his teeth as he felt the physical pain of using more mana than his body had been able to recover.

The chaotic beast took a few steps backward. A green gas came from the wounds on his arm.

Anthony dropped to the landing between the stairs. He started jumping up the stairs as the chaotic beast jumped on the wall, tearing it apart and corrupting the materials there as he rushed for the window Anthony had entered.

Anthony jumped off the stairs, imbued with Bruce's strength as Solomon appeared under the chaotic beast, screaming at them as he threw them off the wall.

"Familiar weakling!" the chaotic beast cursed out as they raked their claws across Solomon.

Solomon cried out, but his mask face only seemed to demonify more as a blade of shadows struck the chaotic beast, making them cry out. Solomon disappeared in smoke, as if he were never there.

Anthony brought the pommel of his sword down and smashed it into the back of the chaotic beast, sending it shooting into the floor. Anthony touched the ceiling and then dug his sword into the wall as he fell, controlling his descent as the stunned chaotic beast started to get up.

Anthony shot past the chaotic beast as a cloud of green appeared above it, followed with a scream of pain. Anthony opened his visor and stuffed the arm into his armor as it started to dissolve into mana, in an effort to replenish his own mana.

Anthony took the other arm and then the legs of the chaotic beast.

"What kind of monster takes his prisoner's limbs!" the elf cried out. As his power decreased, he could no longer hold onto his beast form completely.

"Oh, I'm much smarter than that, wee beastie." Anthony waved his sword at the chaotic beast as he picked up a leg. The green miasma was forcefully dragged in by Anthony and his aura grew quickly.

"You can refine chaos!" The chaotic beast had shown anger and annoyance so far, but now he showed fear.

"Tasty." Anthony dropped the limb. It hit the ground and shattered, turning into dust.

Anthony picked up the next limb and started to drain it as well.

"You—how could you know that? Only the upper echelons of the Guardians could do that!"

"Seems like you chaotic types have been talking a lot about us while it seems that the rest of Dena forgot all about us. Do you have a fan club for the best Guardians? You must." Anthony laughed as he took the last limb and consumed it.

It fell to the ground as dust. Anthony consumed the one inside his armor and shook his leg, dust falling on the floor.

"That's going to be annoying to clean," Anthony complained as he stretched. He felt *good*—better than he had in a long time. He still felt as though he was much weaker than when he was at his peak, but now his mana had recovered quickly. He hadn't been able to fill it yet.

If I can find a few places with a high mana concentration, or some chaotic individuals... Anthony would have licked his lips if he had a tongue.

Guards rushed the stairwell, pointing their weapons at Anthony and the chaotic beast that was shuddering between his beast form and elven form.

"Put your weapons down!" one of the guards yelled.

"Official Guardian business here." Anthony reached his hand out to the side, closing his hand around a gavel that formed from purple energy. His emblem appeared on the left breastplate of his armor.

"I charge you for trespassing on the lands of Dena, for instigating a plague in Skalafell." Anthony brought the hammer down. It rang out and a wave of force pushed the guards back out of the top of the stairwell as the chaotic beast, without his limbs, was suspended in the air. Judges appeared at their podiums in the large hallway that looked cramped with them all in it and the guards who had been ignored and pushed back.

"Hmm?" The pig kin looked around as he scratched his belly.

"Found him," Anthony said to all of the judges.

"This is Skalafell!"

"Silence in the courts!" the pig kin yelled out in an almost bored tone. The pressure of his bloodline made the guard commander slam into the ground face-first.

The guards all lowered their weapons and looked at one another.

"You're guards of the kin! Act like it in a court of law!" The pig kin seemed to have passed his point of patience with his own people.

Anthony took his seat as they all looked at the chaotic beast.

"Oh Leadio." The elf among the court sighed.

The chaotic beast twitched at the name.

"He was once part of our people." The elf judge raised their hand; the right side remained a beast while the left side was elf.

The elf held a deep disappointment in his eyes.

"For creating a plague and setting it upon the population of Skalafell, how do you plead?" Anthony asked.

"Guilty!"

"For trying to kill the people of Dena, how do you plead?"

"Guilty!"

"What was your plan?"

"The plague hides a curse. We weakened the people in the noble houses, made them hide away. Then the people who were poor—we didn't get too many of them—stir the pot with a few people who we had made deals with. Then they would make the poor fight the nobles, then with one another. When the city was opened, the curse would die out. There would be people dead all over the place, but people would learn from the survivors about people turning on one another. We would plant evidence that the elves in the Deepwood were fighting for the humans, add them into the war against the humans," the elf answered.

"How many agents of chaos that are able to convert others are there here or chaotic beasts that have been altered already?" the elemental judge asked.

"There are three more enlightened. Chaotic beasts as you say."

"Where is the agent that changed you?" Anthony asked.

"I do not know. I was given my mission and the curse, that was all."

"Chaos cell." The gnome sighed.

The others looked at the split man.

"It would be good if we could trace out the cell and see who they're connected to but then the plague will advance too much," the dwarf said.

"Guardian Anthony?" the pig kin asked Anthony.

"I say that we destroy the cell here, then we alert the authorities in the area. Make sure that the people are prepared to deal with chaotic agents if they want to return here," Anthony said.

"With the power of the chaotic forces, do you think that you will be able to heal the city?" the elf asked.

The judges all looked to Anthony.

Anthony let out a sigh. "I'm not sure. Once the curse is removed, then people will be able to heal instead of getting sicker. From there, I can clean the water and use my spells to enhance its ability to heal. I will need to help here and there with the most severe cases. There will be people who could die, but then medicines will work on them unlike before when they were affected by the curse."

"The sooner the better." The hob tapped their shamanic staff on the ground.

"I ask the court to allow me to examine the accused's memories," Anthony said.

"It will wipe their personality and kill them." The pig kin looked to the elf.

"This is a war and they have attacked our people. They don't care about their methods and we must eliminate their chaos so that it doesn't affect Dena. He has become interconnected with chaos. There is no way to remove the power from him without destroying him."

Anthony could see the pain in the elf's eyes as he said those words.

The chaotic beast was trying to move against invisible restraints.

"I put it to a vote," Anthony said.

They all cast their votes anonymously.

"Everyone is in agreement." He looked at the results. "Leadio, your memories will be scanned, your mind destroyed, and your power will be converted so that it might no longer stain Dena."

The hammer hit the surface of his table.

His table disappeared and Anthony stepped forward through the purple court. He stepped upon the air. As he reached the accused, he put his hand on the man's head. Purple and white intermixed. Anthony was hit with a blast of memories. A young man growing up, he hadn't been outstanding but he had a simple family who lived on the outskirts of Dena. He had been out playing when a group of beast kin had hidden in his village. They had been across the border in the human lands; the elves didn't know and hosted them, looking after their wounds.

Humans had come in and demanded to be allowed into the town.

With ancient elven culture, the mayor refused politely. The beast kin were their guests; they wouldn't go against their old traditions.

The humans had then burned down the village. The beast kin and humans had fought one another. The beast kin had won, but instead of helping the people who had helped them, they had taken supplies from the elves and ran off.

He came back to find his mother, father, and sister killed. He didn't know whether it was by the beast kin or the humans. He didn't care; he wanted to destroy them both.

He grew up, no longer the carefree boy from before. He trained in the art of fighting. He looked to increase his strength. He wanted to go and fight the beasts and the humans, to show them the power of the elves to get them to pay for the deaths of his family. He was a proud elf and he knew that one day they would step on these other races and thrash them, like a grandfather would teach his disobedient grandson, and then they would come to learn the errors of their ways, submitting themselves to the elves freely, entering into a prosperous time.

Time went on and he applied to the military. He wanted to be on the border patrols and he made it in. He was an angry man, but toward the elves he was civil, turning his anger outward.

He watched the borders, watched the beast kin and the humans, seeing what they did to one another. He asked to go and lead raiding parties into their lands. He butted heads with the leadership.

He realized that the elves were weak. They looked good and they were strong, but they were unwilling to use that strength against others. He became disillusioned with the greatness of the elven race.

He found the aftermath of a raid. There had been elves in the city, trading with humans when beast kin had raided.

He saw the state of the elves and he led a group of his followers to hunt down the beast kin, killing them for their crimes.

He was dismissed from the military, but escaped being imprisoned. He left the Deepwood and headed to the lands of the humans and beast kin. He started to kill people on both sides because he felt like it. He was found by someone—a gnome—protected and given targets.

He was introduced to others who thought like him, then the Agents of Chaos, who had unlocked power from another world that allowed them massive power. That was how they were getting the beast kin and the humans to fight against one another.

He was accepted, others agreed to his viewpoints. They looked up to him, instead of giving him looks of disdain; it felt good. His path and decisions right.

"Leadio, you've been picked directly by a true Agent of Chaos. He has a mission for you and your people," the gnome who had mentored him said.

"I live to serve," Leadio said, a fervent belief in his eyes. He *craved* to prove himself to those higher than him, in a way that he had never found when he was in the military.

"You are going to head to Skalafell. You will start a plague there, cursing those in the city. With this, you will plant evidence that it was the elves fighting for the humans. Finally you will be able to show the elves the truth of the humans and the beast kin, have them step out of the Deepwood and finally step on the two races," the gnome said, his eyes glowing.

Leadio's body shook in agitation that ran from the base of his spine to his mind. He felt determination, happiness, and relief. Everything that he had been doing for his entire life led up to this point.

Anthony saw his conspirators. One of them had been with Leadio when they hunted down the beast kin.

They had reunited and been directly blessed by an Agent of Chaos, going through a ritual that twisted their bodies. It was incredibly painful as everything that they were was twisted into something new. It was needed to cast such a powerful curse and to make sure that they had the power to deal with their tasks.

Anthony stared into the depths of the man, a man who was just a boy looking to get back at those who tore his life apart, who took the goodwill of his parents, his family, and all those he knew, and destroyed it.

In everyone's life, in everyone's mind, they are not the bad person; they're the person fighting for what is right. It is slowly over time that their morals are eroded and that their mind can be changed and altered, going from trying to get justice for his parents to instigating a horrendous crime against the innocent to embroil his entire race into a war that would lead to the destruction of untold towns like his own and other families.

Anthony opened his eyes. There was no anger there, just sadness, seeing Leadio's life. He wished he could have been there to make it better, to help a lost child.

He looked at Leadio. His head was to the side, his eyes blank as he was now reliving his life in spurts, laughing and then crying, then thrashing around, the memories all jumbled together, now losing his touch on time and when he existed.

Anthony cast a spell on his hand and held Leadio's head. "Find peace, Leadio," he said under his breath. A white spell formation appeared on Leadio's head. His face went slack as the power in his body turned into a storm of power clashing with one another. It drained out of his corpse, collecting into Anthony's hand.

Anthony felt the rush of energy that filled his own mana reserves. He had been powered by the heart in his chest as he had drained his mana again and again, causing him to lose bone mass and degrade with time. His yellowed and cracked bones now started to repair, thickening to normal proportions, and his eyes glowed brighter. His yellowing bones started to turn whiter as the familiar runes on his body deepened, in color radiating a powerful might.

Anthony converted all of the energy from Leadio, feeling stronger than he ever had before.

"Solomon, find them." Anthony shared all of his memories with his familiars so Solomon didn't need to know anymore. The shadows around Anthony fled.

"We will see you shortly," the pig kin judge said as the courtroom disappeared.

Dave's wings reached out of Anthony's back. The sunlight arched over the city, shining through the broken window, catching Anthony's armor and Dave's flapping wings, the tree carved into the back of his armor visible to all.

"Make sure that Count Lemar does not leave. Capture these people." Anthony took out a piece of paper and wrote down several names. "Lady Tissis is not to leave the castle. She will stand trial to see what role she played in this all. Today, Skalafell will be cleansed of corruption, both from within and those who manipulated it." Anthony released the list and it floated toward the guard who had been slammed into the ground.

Anthony looked back at them all. "Hear my orders, guards of Skalafell. If one innocent is harmed, if one conspirator escapes, I will hold you all responsible." He let his words hang in the air.

Anthony felt Solomon signaling to him; he flapped his wings and raced for the open window. "Today is the day you prove you wear that armor not just for the money, but for the responsibility that comes with it!"

He shot through the window and up into the sky, his speed much faster than before as he rose up above the city.

***

"What is that?"

"Is that a star?"

Some of the workers standing outside of the city looked up. They had been working all night to make sure that the people of Skalafell had clean food and water.

Aila looked up with Tommie, seeing the glowing star that seemed to rise above the city.

"Is that a person?"

"How can that be? They're much too small."

"It looks like a knight? A human knight?"

"Are they attacking?"

"How could that be possible here?" another said.

"They must be like one of those angels," someone else said in a whisper.

"An angel?"

They started to talk among themselves, but Aila could feel that instead of being scared, they were hopeful.

Aila and Tommie stood back from it all, looking up at that glowing figure with golden wings.

"It's a Guardian," Aila said. She didn't know why but there were tears in her eyes as she looked up at him. She felt as if everything would be okay, seeing him standing over the city.

He tilted forward and dropped, shooting toward the ground and disappearing from sight.

Tommie and Aila looked at each other. They would be able to identify that knight anywhere.

"We've still got work to do," Aila said.

"He can't do it all on his own." Tommie grinned.

The two of them turned back to their own tasks.

"Come on! Get those supplies on the pallets!" Aila yelled.

"Those masks need more charcoal. Someone run down to the legionnaires and get some more sand for the filters!" Tommie said.

Chapter: Running Scared

Lady Tissis sat in her office. She was looking at the list that Anthony had made and passed to her guards.

They had found her tied up right away. Hearing all of the events, she couldn't help but be shocked. When she saw the body of Leadio, who had returned to his elven form, she confirmed that it was the man who had been in her room.

She learned that he had been with Count Lemar, her brother-in-law. She couldn't and didn't want to deal with it, so she had him sent to the dungeon.

The list of names were Lemar's closest allies, as well as different people from the underworld of Skalafell. Listed beside their names was the crimes that they stood accused of.

"Rescind my previous orders. Use all of the power of the guards to arrest these individuals." Tissis gritted her teeth as she passed the list over to her guard captain.

"Yes, my lady."

She could tell that he was pleased to not carry out her last orders.

He saluted Lady Tissis and left the room quickly.

Skalafell was fated to be a busy place in the coming days. The guards gathered in the castle rushed out on their mounted beasts, wearing their full armor as they went into the slums, to root out the underworld figures and to the noble houses to gather up Lemar's people.

The Black Rags assisted instead of hindered as they heard that the information had come from their leader.

The slums were peaceful as the guards who wouldn't have entered before went in and came out without issue.

Tissis looked out of her window as people came and left. She didn't have the energy or mental capacity to do anything more. She saw the city—the people moving around, the guards leaving and coming back, a flash of light in the distance. She wondered whether it was Guardian Anthony.

"Another report of Guardian Anthony being sighted. A building was destroyed and a secret entrance into the sewers found. There were seventeen people who were found unconscious, bound with metal, with 'suspect' written on their heads. We have since taken them into custody," a messenger said.

"Very well." Tissis coughed, trying to stifle it as she waved the messenger away.

As the door closed, she let out the coughs. Her whole body was weak and covered in a cold sweat by the time she was done. She forced herself to breathe.

My fate and the fate of the city now rests in Guardian Anthony's hands. She didn't like having to rely on someone else, but there was nothing that she could do. *If I may die, at least I die doing what I believe in.* She mustered her strength and left her office, feeling tired and drained from the long night. She walked through the castle, to her room.

She opened the door and walked in, seeing him still in his feeble state. She walked over to him and took a cloth from the servants.

"Take the day off," she said to them.

"But, Lady Tissis..." The head servant spoke up.

"You've done more than enough. Please," Tissis said.

Seeing the look in her eyes, the head servant bowed. "Please call if you need anything, my lady."

Tissis nodded and then looked at the guards.

"We'll wait outside," one of them said.

Tissis gave them a small smile as they left the room, leaving her alone with her husband for the first time in weeks.

She wetted the cloth and pressed it to his head, then his neck and his chest. She could feel his body burning up, see his ribs poking through.

He seemed to sense her there as he nudged her hip with his snout. She looked to see him staring up at her.

Her heart felt as if it were being clenched. "It'll all be okay, love," she whispered to him as she dabbed his face.

He closed his eyes and fell back to sleep.

Tissis, feeling tired, laid down in the bed beside him, holding him close. She closed her eyes as well, a wave of fatigue settling over her.

***

Anthony walked through the street. Behind him, there were three chaotic beasts with their arms and legs tied as he dragged them toward the central square.

As he walked through the streets, people looked from their windows and started to enter the streets, talking about the leader of the Black Rags, Guardian Anthony—talking about what had been going on in the city since the early morning.

People gathered; Black Rags appeared and they made sure the people remained orderly and that they didn't crowd Anthony and his payload.

He reached the central square, where a number of guards waited.

"Bring out the accused. We'll have their trial in front of the people of Skalafell for all to see and hear," Anthony said.

The guard commander nodded and sent out a messenger.

Anthony waited, gathering his mana.

The guard captain arrived and a number of armored carriages descended from the castle.

He spoke quietly to Anthony. "Lady Tissis has fallen into a deep sleep. We can't wake her. I am the legal guardian for Keze, so I am currently running the city. I don't want to say anything that might panic the people," the guard captain said.

Anthony gritted his teeth and nodded. "We'll deal with the accused. Then I can break the curse and look to heal them."

The guard captain looked into his glowing orbs before he let out a sigh. "Don't betray my trust." His statement was equal parts threat and promise.

Anthony nodded and then the guard captain stood to the side.

Anthony stepped forward in front of the people; his gavel appeared in his hand.

"He really can summon a purple hammer!" a younger member of the crowd called out to their friends.

"Is he going to call in the judges?" another asked in a shocked voice.

Anthony brought down his hammer and it sounded out over the crowd, breaking the conversations. All eyes were on Anthony as purple lines flowed out of where the hammer hit, forming the benches and table for the judges as well as their seats.

Purple miasma rolled together, and then dispersed, revealing the six other judges in their purple robes with their Guardian emblem. They took their seats.

There was an inviolable aura around them as they looked down at the trio floating up into the air, standing in front of the court as they regained their senses.

The first thing that the people of Dena turned chaotic beasts saw was a grand purple courtroom, with seven judges looking at them with hardened expressions.

"Read out the charges!" the elemental said. Their body of twisting wind and lightning made all shiver when looking at the concentrated destruction.

"Malik of Jorsen, Faromeer of the Lizet Isles, Tsarra of Asryennas, you stand accused of crimes against the people of Dena. For conspiring and carrying out an attack on Skalafell, creating and propagating a plague and a curse in an effort to incite chaos, war, and bloodshed. For attacking the innocent and working with Agents of Chaos to gain power to do so. You stand accused of murder, bribery, torture in the case of Tsarra. And working against the people of Dena, aiding the enemy forces of chaos. Your trial will now begin!" the gnome judge read out. His size might have been diminutive, but none dared to look down on him as he read the charges.

***

Tysien was in the crowd as she watched the trio's charges. Malik and Faromeer were both from the beast kin race; Tsarra was elven.

Hearing their crimes, she couldn't help but stare at them, looking at their elvish or beast kin appearance.

They look so normal, just like someone you would see on the street—you would never know the difference. Anthony might be a human but he has only had the best of intentions for the people of Dena, for the people of Skalafell.

The crimes of the trio were confirmed and the entire crowd was against them. This plague had hit people from across the city. It didn't matter one's position or what power they had; all of them had been affected in some way. They stood shoulder to shoulder, looking at the accused.

Anthony stepped forward, reaching out his hand and placing it on Tsarra.

"Chaos will come for you all!" she yelled out, a crazed look on her face.

"It is welcome to, as I hunt the chaos," Anthony said as magical power blazed in his hand.

Tsarra's crazed eyes turned dull as she started to cry, then laugh, then scream out, her mind broken into fragments. Those watching looked on in horror.

The other two who had stood tall, seeing how Tsarra had been broken, started to struggle against their bindings.

Anthony repeated his actions on Faromeer.

"Please, no! No! I can do better! I can change!" Malik yelled out.

"Sometimes people are too far past redemption." Anthony's voice was dull, tired, and pained as he reached out.

Malik's head dropped forward as he started to laugh, as if he had heard the best joke ever.

Anthony stood in front of them and raised his hands. Their expressions stilled and their heads dropped forward as they died.

Anthony withdrew the chaotic energy from them all. The pressure and corruption that had been affecting everyone's bloodlines and the mana of the area relaxed.

The three bodies were taken away.

Anthony took his seat in the court. "We will have a short recess before continuing."

The judge's tables wrapped up, hiding everything from view.

They were like that for five minutes before a large spell formation appeared over the courtroom. It grew larger, with interconnecting magical circles growing and settling over Skalafell.

Everyone watched in awe.

This kind of spell, it must be a tier-six spell!

The power in the spell formation was consumed, leaving a powerful orb in the sky. It was blue in color and lightning danced on its surface. It dropped to the ground. People let out a gasp as it touched the ground and detonated.

A wall of light shot through the city; people screamed as it passed through homes and buildings as if they didn't exist. Though instead of being hurt, people felt the power moving through their body but didn't notice any changes.

The courtroom unfolded once again and the judges were visible.

Tysien thought that they looked less life-like, as if the power holding them there had weakened.

"Next!" Anthony said.

People started to move around as they realized that they were okay. They had more questions than answers as they looked up at the judges.

Anthony cleared his throat as people started to get rowdy.

"That was a spell to break the curse that was affecting everyone. With the curse now lifted, you will be able to use healing spells or medical concoctions and they should work. Guards, bring me barrels of fresh filtered water."

Guards looked to the guard captain, who nodded to them.

They came back a few minutes later.

The elven judge stood over the barrels and used a spell on the water.

"Distribute the water to the people here and then pass to the Black Rags to distribute," Anthony said.

Again the guards looked at their guard captain.

"Get to it," the guard captain said.

The guards took the water and started to distribute it as people moved forward to have this blessed water.

Anthony's hammer smacked on the table and everyone calmed down and looked at him.

"Form lines. Only one serving per person. You don't need any more," Anthony said.

People were organized and those who had the water started to head home to tell others and bring them to the square.

"The next accused," Anthony said, looking at the guard captain.

People were brought out of their carriages one by one to stand in front of the judges.

"Please don't kill me!" a large panther kin with a scar down the side of his face said.

"The judgement passed down must be agreed upon by the court. The death penalty is rare," the pig kin said.

Tysien was at the back of the crowd as people were brought out into the court. Many of them were innocent of their crimes; they had been unwittingly used as part of the ploy. As more people were brought forward, a story was revealed.

The Agents of Chaos were brought into the city by an underground group who set them up with different hidden locations. They also got them access to the city. The Agents of Chaos had made contact with people inside the city. For months, they had been building their power base. They promised Count Lemar and those who were displeased with the state of Skalafell the position of city lord. The city lord would die and then they would take over. To show their magnanimity, they would then uncover the elven plot and build people's anger toward the people in the Deepwood.

Some were just treacherous; others actively knew that the poison was due to them. They used it on the rival noble families and then spread it through the streets with their carriages.

They were people of Skalafell and the beast kin, so although their crimes were revealed to all, Anthony left their punishment to be determined by the beast kin judicial system at a later date. They were all bound with the purple chains to make sure that they wouldn't be able to get away.

People from Skalafell were coming to drink the cleansing water. People on stretchers were brought out by the Black Rags; others took the barrels of cleansing water and distributed it to those who weren't strong enough to leave their homes.

The crimes were read out as the judges and Anthony worked tirelessly. They went through tens of people before Count Lemar was brought onto the stage. At this point, everyone knew the crimes he had committed by his conspirators' confessions.

"Count Lemar." Anthony looked at the man. He stood tall, no regret in his eyes as he looked Anthony in the eyes, defiant.

"You are accused of working with Agents of Chaos against the people of Dena, for breaking your vow and the vow of your family to assist and help those under the protection of Skalafell. You are accused of poisoning your brother and the people of Skalafell." Anthony sounded tired reading out the charges. "How do you plead?"

"Guilty."

"For what reasons did you carry out this malicious act?" Anthony looked on Count Lemar. The courtyard was largely silent, all straining to listen.

Count Lemar's eyes were in a daze, but there was a sneer on his face. "City lord, that dog? That was meant to be my position! My father took him in and gave him our resources, but he forgets his position! Standing above me, taking the woman I love! I would remove him from power, take his seat. Then I would be able to slowly take his wife for my own. I would right how I was wronged and take back the position I deserve! He looked down on me, would send over gifts for the family, make it seem like he was a caring, brotherly figure but he was just doing it to shame me!"

The dazed look disappeared. As he looked around, there was no repentance on his face.

People in the crowd barely held onto their anger. Anthony and the judges glanced at them all, silencing them.

"Count Lemar, your crimes are grave and I don't know if there is a way that you can possibly atone for them." The pig kin's voice sounded like distant thunder; people felt their bloodlines quivering.

"Your personal fate will be figured out by the people of Dena. As a clan spirit, I render this judgement." The pig kin looked at the other judges; they gestured that they would take a step backward.

"You have stained your very bloodline. From now on, you and your conspirators will no longer stain the great heritage of your bloodline." The pig kin clan spirit held out his hand.

Those already charged let out pained noises. Count Lemar coughed blood and dropped to his knees, a look of panic in his eyes.

The pig kin twisted his hand and pulled. Blood was spat from the different accused's mouths. The blood mist formed different beasts in mid-air and they all rushed toward the pig kin's hand.

They gathered together, galloping or roaming around the pig kin, who lowered his hand. "You will remain kin-less. Any children you sire will not have their ancestors' bloodline."

The mist beasts took off into the skies. Lemar seemed to shrink as his powerful body was greatly weakened.

Tysien and the other beast kin in the square all felt a chill run through them.

Someone can remove a bloodline like that? With being unable to pass on their bloodline, their later generations will never be able to increase their strength. They will have to pass a bloodline trial in order to get a bloodline, which is incredibly difficult and there is a high chance of dying.

"This brings our court to a close." Anthony stood. He looked at the people in the square. "Black Rags, make sure that the water gets to the worst affected first and tell the medical staff that they should start using their spells and concoctions to help those in the open-air hospitals."

The city had largely fallen under the Black Rags' control. Working with the guards, they could distribute the cleansing water the fastest.

Did he have this in mind when he created the Black Rags? Tysien moved forward. She was verified by the guards and she took barrels, loading them onto her mount. They rushed off to one of the open-air hospitals that was farther away.

She saw a messenger running at full speed, reaching the guard captain and forcing out his words.

A look of panic appeared on his face as he ran up to Anthony.

They jumped onto beasts. The guards released their reins as they raced up the streets toward the castle. The guard captain's voice boomed through the streets, madness in his eyes.

Chapter: A New Skalafell

Anthony let out a sigh as he pinched the front of his helmet. He looked over to the guard captain and shook his head.

The guard captain set his jaw and looked at the door.

Keze was on the other side of the door, playing with her maids, not sure what all the commotion was about.

"She must've got more of the plague than we thought. She fell into a sleep, tired from it all," Anthony said.

She looked so peaceful lying beside her husband. His breathing had leveled out and he was showing signs of recovery.

"The city lord?" the guard captain asked.

"He'll survive," Anthony confirmed and stood up.

Some servants were in the corner, crying to one another.

"Thank you," the guard captain said.

Anthony nodded and headed out of the room.

"Hey, you're the tree knight!" Keze said as he exited the room.

Anthony's heart twisted as he looked over at the girl. She was half hiding behind one of her maids, who were looking at Anthony to pick out clues of what was happening behind the door.

"That I am, little miss," Anthony said.

"My mommy said that you might look all scary but that you're really working hard to help out people," Keze said.

Anthony stood there, not sure what to say. "That's kind of her to say," he finally choked out.

"I'm sorry if I made any trouble," Keze said with an uneasy expression. She held her hands behind her back as she moved back and forth.

"It's all okay now." Anthony couldn't even picture how crushed she would be in just minutes. He wanted to hug her and protect her from that pain, but he knew that he wouldn't be able to.

Keze beamed as she looked at Anthony.

"Stay strong, little one," Anthony said in a small voice. He took one last look at her before he turned and walked away.

An image appeared in his mind's eye, of a man and a woman who had died defending the other. A simple cloak covered them both as a younger Anthony dropped to his knees. There were no tears, no feelings—just noise in his head. He'd snuck out and had been wandering around, knowing he needed to go home but he didn't want to face his parents' anger. He knew they would be okay after some time.

He had been thinking of what he would say to them when he ran into a ranger who was friends with his parents. He took him back to their isolated home when he saw the door smashed open.

He found Anthony's parents and put his cloak over them.

Anthony felt like it was a dream, as if it couldn't possibly be real.

Anthony headed out of the castle and Solomon appeared.

"Take me to the worst cases," Anthony said in a grim voice.

He rode on the mount he had come in on.

Solomon guided him through the city. Anthony expended his mana again and again, recovering while he was on his mount, moving across Skalafell to render aid to those he could.

***

Ex-Count Lemar sat in his cell, looking at the bars. He had been doing this for the people, doing this for justice. His brother had to have used underhanded methods to get his position, to make Tissis his wife.

Why was it that he took everything that I desire? Still, he is too far gone and I have been giving him more poison every time I see him with the healing concoctions I provided. No healer should be able to save him now.

There was a vindictive light in his eyes as he heard the door to the dungeon open. He looked up as he saw the guard captain appear.

"Come to beat a count?" Lemar sneered.

"Tissis died from the plague."

Those five words were more powerful than losing his bloodline.

Lemar's thoughts turned chaotic as the guard captain left.

"You're lying! I didn't poison her!" Lemar jumped up and grabbed the bars.

"You brought the plague into the city, these Agents of Chaos. Does it matter? You'll stand trial for her murder." The guard captain continued to walk.

"I didn't want her to die! I loved her!"

"No, you just wanted to have what your brother had, while he only wanted your recognition." The guard captain had served three city lords, had looked after their families and come to know them closely. He barely contained his rage as Lemar was left there in shock and pain.

"You're lying!" Lemar yelled, grabbing and shaking the bars. He felt as though he was losing his mind. "Come back here and tell the truth!" Lemar screamed out as the door closed and locked. Lemar continued yelling but there were no answers.

***

Tommie rubbed his face, covered in dirt and grime. He needed a bath and sleep. Like everyone else, he had seen the wall of light that had spread through Skalafell. They had sent in messages, fearing that it was some kind of attack spell.

They got mixed messages, telling them about a trial, then about a curse being lifted.

As more messages went back and forth, they started to get a clear idea of what was happening in the city.

In the last two days since the end of the trial, the Black Rags and the guards had been working together, bringing supplies to those in need, caring for the worst affected, organizing funerals.

For some, the cure didn't come soon enough, but it looked like the majority of people would recover.

As people were healed, they would then turn around and help out the Black Rags. Supplies were distributed fairly to the nobles and the common folk.

The legion kept on helping with the traders.

They were shipping in their own medical supplies as they were helping those affected.

Anthony ran from place to place. He had gone through several mounts. The guards and Black Rags worked together to get him to the sickest people. He would heal them so that they had a higher chance of surviving, then flop onto his mount and go to the next place.

It was unknown how many people he had used his healing spells on.

He consumed mana-concentrated training aids as if they were candy. There were fewer people who needed aid as time went on and Anthony's critical heals weren't needed that much.

"Gnome, we have an issue with one of the winches!" a beast kin said.

"Coming," Tommie said. His whole body was aching, his skin itchy and unwashed but he didn't stop working.

***

Anthony sat on Skalafell's wall. Solomon appeared beside him before disappearing into his leg.

He stood and stretched as he saw Tysien approaching with the leaders of the Black Rags. The guard captain was with them.

"Everything going well?" Anthony asked.

"People are recovering across the city. With the curse lifted, people are able to begin healing. The plague is under control and people should be back to normal in a few days. We've been talking to the legion. They're going to send in some people to check on people's conditions. Then they can allow us to open the city gates and they'll take the accused to Bracegar, where all of the clans are and their sentences will be given out," Tysien said.

"Looks like you've got everything sorted." Anthony nodded.

"Thank you for your help," the guard captain said.

"I didn't do much. These three did much more than me, and didn't sleep much the entire time." Anthony looked at Ubi, Mai, and Jun, who still wore their Black Rags. But they had them around their necks instead of covering their faces.

The trio had a mix of emotions on their faces before they bowed.

"Thank you for placing your trust in us and guiding us!" Jun yelled out so his voice wouldn't get choked up.

"Come on, guys. I might have helped you a little bit, but you put in the work," Anthony said.

The trio slowly came out of their bow.

"What do we do with the Black Rags now?" Mai asked.

"Help the people of Dena and Skalafell. There won't always be a plague but if you can help one another, you can become stronger than before. If it stays around, make sure that you are a force of good, or disband the group," Anthony said.

Ubi, Jun, and Mai clasped their fists as there was a noise from the other side of the wall.

"Seems it's about time to go. Watch out—there are forces of chaos in the shadows and it looks like they're ramping up their efforts," Anthony said as he walked toward the other side of the wall.

"Stay classy." Anthony tripped and fell over the wall. He let out a shriek as he windmilled his arms and legs, slamming into the ground.

"Could you stop falling all over the place," Aila hissed as she looked around.

"I didn't mean to." Anthony pushed up off the ground, mud stuck in his helmet.

Aila gave Anthony a skeptical look. "Come on, let's go," Aila said finally.

"A nice comfortable bed, a warm path, and stew—I could go for some stew. Nice and thick broth, with big chunks of meat and veggies," Tommie said.

"Hello to you, too, my gnomish friend," Anthony said, and looked at Aila.

"Hey Anthony, wake me up when we get there." Tommie leaned forward and little snoring sounds came from him.

"Hasn't slept most of the time," Aila explained.

"Sleep riding—this should be good. Aren't we going on the road again? Why is he talking about warm water?" Anthony patted old Ramona, who let out a pleased noise as he got up into his saddle and they started forward.

"Well, I might not have told him that we're going right back on the road to not draw attention," Aila said awkwardly in her low voice.

Tommie snorted, muttering in his sleep. "No, that's too much, need more charcoal."

Anthony turned and waved to the people on the wall. "Not the most elegant departure. Thought it would be kind of badass," Anthony muttered.

"There is nothing graceful about you, Anthony." Aila leaned forward, lying on her beast. "Keep watch."

"Just because I don't need sleep doesn't mean I want to take watch every time," Anthony complained. He looked over.

Aila was already asleep.

"Well, Ramona, it's just you and me! So how have you and the twins been? Have you been eating well?" Anthony asked in a dopey voice as he gave Ramona scratches.

Chapter: Beauty Isn't Skin Deep

Claire read over the reports. She looked more lethargic than she had in hundreds of years as she rubbed her eye sockets.

"It looks like the forces of chaos are moving again. They're also converting more people into chaotic beasts. They must be trying to put their plans into action before the coming battle." She looked ahead and tapped her finger on her armrest.

The knight standing in the room fell over onto the ground.

"Damien, you were standing still. How did you trip?" she yelled.

"Sorry. I was just, umm..." Damien laughed awkwardly and started to get back up.

"Battle nut," Claire muttered. "The good thing is that while the Agents of Chaos have tried to enter Ilsal, none of them have been able to affect our cities. The main problems lay in the main continent. There are forces of chaos manipulating the war between the humans and beasts. It looks like they're making an effort to cause inner issues with the beast kin and draw the elves into the fight." Claire sat back in her chair.

"Send out some of our judiciaries to Epan. We've secured our position here. Let's see if we can root out the forces of chaos. As they're more active, they'll mess up more," Claire said.

"What about...*him*?" Damien asked.

"Leave him to his own devices. He might be as dull as your hammer at times, but he usually ambles his way through." Claire sighed but the corners of her mouth lifted slightly.

***

Tommie woke up early. Anthony had found them a place to camp late into the night. The two others had sleepily tossed out their bedrolls and collapsed, but Tommie hadn't even made it into his bedroll.

Tommie had a busting need to relieve himself and he ran through some trees. The relaxing sounds of water hitting ground filled the air as Tommie let out a satisfied sigh.

He finished up his business and he saw the sunlight touching the water through the trees.

Tommie felt at peace. As he saw that water, he could feel his itchy skin and his need to wash. He went back, grabbing a towel and soap.

He stripped down to his underwear and jumped in. He rubbed his face and body quickly as he felt his skin turning to goose bumps with the cold lake water.

Damn, that's refreshing! Tommie surfaced. He heard Anthony whistling, so he turned around, seeing a skeleton washing his bones.

"AHHHHYAHH!! SKELETON!"

Birds fled for safety and deer were startled into motion as a flailing gnome sped toward the shore.

The skeleton cried out, covering their bones, "Where! Where are they?"

Tommie wasn't making it very far and the skeleton calmed down.

"What are you flailing around for, Tommie?" Anthony's voice came from the skeleton.

"What did you do to Anthony?" Tommie demanded. He now had his feet underneath him and was trying to force his way to shore.

"How could I do anything to myself? Tommie, you sound ridiculous!" Anthony walked out of the water. His heart was beating away and his bones sparkled in the early morning sunlight.

"He is an upright human and you're an undead!" Tommie drew out his small sword from its scabbard and pointed it at Anthony.

"Ouch, Tommie! Beauty is not skin deep!" Anthony said, hurt as he held one hand up to his shocked jaw. "Put that sword down! You'll hurt someone! It looks like we need to have a talk about beauty. It is not just one's outer appearance but how they are on the inside. See, my inside and outside are the same, so it's easier to love. Come here." Anthony moved toward the gnome.

**

Aila woke up to Tommie's scream and then Anthony yelling. She pulled out her dagger and gathered her mana as she ran toward the noise and the lake.

Rushing out of the trees, ready to fight, she saw Anthony cradling Tommie, who was looking around with wide, alarmed eyes as Anthony patted him.

"It's okay, little fella. You know, some things aren't always as they appear on the outside. I once knew this crossdressing orc—you'd swear that they were a female goblin when they were done. Incredibly good with a bit of mud, some powders, and a brush!"

Tommie let out a squeak as he saw Aila. His eyes pleaded with her. *Are you seeing this?* his eyes seemed to demand.

"What are you washing for?" Aila asked.

"I might be undead but I have standards! My bones got really worn down with the mana loss—look at this yellowing!" Anthony pointed at his femur but Aila couldn't see any difference in color from the rest of his bones.

"Right, well, I'm going to get some breakfast. Don't struggle—cuddle Tommie too much," Aila said, quickly retreating.

"Aila!" Tommie wailed, betrayed by his closest ally.

I don't want to be hugged by a skeleton either! Good luck, young Tommie. She silently saluted the little gnome and then went back to her bedroll, shivering as she thought of what she had just seen.

"It's all just a bad dream," she muttered to herself as she went to sleep.

Chapter: Norlund

Tommie was still casting gazes at Anthony. Since Laisa, he had thought that Anthony was a little eccentric, not needing to eat that much or go to the bathroom. But now that he knew the truth, that Anthony was one of the cursed undead, he was having a little trouble digesting it all.

He is a good person, even if he is only bones and a heart. He has helped a lot of people since I've met him.

"You're going to burn holes in my armor, staring that much. I'm sorry but I'm not into you, Tommie," Anthony said from ahead.

"Who said I was interested!" Tommie said.

Aila snickered at their back and forth, staying out of it.

She seemed perfectly fine. It was clear from her reaction that she had known that Anthony was an undead.

Do they not trust me? Well, I have only just met them; it makes sense that they don't trust me completely. Though he was washing there. Tommie sunk into thought. He didn't notice Anthony as he dropped back.

Anthony cleared his throat, pulling Tommie out of his stream of thought and making him nearly jump off his mount. He moved his arms around, not really sure what they were moving to *do*. When he jumped up, he was caught in his stirrups and fell backward, his arms cartwheeling as he yelled out.

"Overreact a little there?" Anthony asked.

Tommie held his chest, feeling his racing heart as he worked to calm himself.

"So, what's plaguing your mind there, my gnomish companion?" Anthony asked. "Are you having more troubles with the Gnome-inator? No worries, Norlund is one of the largest trading ports this side of the Swirling Seas. I am sure that you will be able to find plenty of parts and things for the Gnome-inator!"

"He's freaked out you're all yellowing bones," Aila said, not looking back as she stretched on her mount and started to brew herself a tea for the morning.

"You know that I'm sensitive about the yellowing!" Anthony complained.

"Well, stop standing out in the moonlight in the nude. Are you trying to make innocent bystanders crap their pants? Or have their hearts fail them?"

"Aila! I am a refinement of the undead form!" Anthony gasped.

"Well, I guess you are technically a body refined into an undead," Aila conceded. She packed her leaves into a contraption and put it into some water, using a fire spell on the underside of the cup to heat it up.

"Truly, you both need remedial lessons on true beauty. You all think that it is all skin deep!" Anthony said.

"And who screams like a scared cat when they see their reflection in the water?" Aila yawned and waved her hand, the fire spell going out on her finger. She sat back in her saddle, moving with her mount, who was eagerly plodding ahead, picking up some roots in his mouth.

Ramona crooned at him.

He looked at her with his big cute lizard eyes, pouting at her.

She made another noise of reprimand as he let go of the roots, snorting at another group of roots that were taunting him.

"How are you able to do all of these things? Aren't undead just fighters?" Tommie asked.

"Well, low-grade undead are like pissed-off toothpick men who attack anything that is in range. I'm a little more refined than that. I'm a death knight, pretty badass. Though I can use my familiars because they are soul bound to me, so alive or undead I can use them. Though if I was to die and my soul to disperse, then the bindings between my familiars and me would be broken. Though I need a higher mana capacity than what I have right now to wake them all up. I can only use a few of them at the same time and it burns through my mana like you would not believe and there is no mana savings time on this!" Anthony complained.

"So how do you increase your mana capacity?"

"Well, I need to refill it. The elves increase their mana by cultivating it, right? Well, I need to do something similar. I absorb in mana; that increases my capacity and then once I have done that, I can draw in mana to fill that capacity much faster!"

"Think of it like a balloon: once you blow it up the first time, it is easier to blow it up a second time," Aila said from ahead.

"It's just been awhile since I blew up this balloon so it's being a bit of a pain, though the more times I use mana, the more it's forcefully expanded," Anthony said.

"Where do you hold your mana in all of that?"

"I 'unno. I just use the stuff." Anthony shrugged.

"You magical races." Tommie shook his head. "Using massive power that can change the world around you and you know next to nothing about it!"

"Well, do you want to go and study in a library? Practical knowledge is the future, my boy! Look, on your resume, you went to the library, did a bit of school—you think that will look better than saying you went on a grand adventure? Seeing the *world,* the people, and the miracles that exist within it? Searching out the mysteries and finding yourself? What do you think that the person hiring you would say?"

"You should have stayed in school, you hippie," Tommie said.

"Ugh, gnomes and your logic. Gotta live a little, Tommie!"

Tommie blinked a few times and shook his head. "I can't believe I'm being told to live a little by an undead skeleton."

"And what does that tell you?"

Tommie tried to figure out the hidden meaning in Anthony's words. "What does it mean?"

"I have no clue. I was hoping you knew," Anthony said. "Nice pair of fields you have there!"

Aila sighed and shook her head as she drank her tea.

They emerged from the tree line, passing a low wall. Fields stretched across the land. They went up a little rise. There were fields for miles around, creating a horseshoe shape around a large city. The city stood on the edge of the land. It was circular, with walls that appeared atop small islands dotted around the outside of the harbor city.

"Norlund," Aila said.

There were white masts coming in as massive ships entered the harbors, passing those great walls.

Other ships were leaving, heading to cities up and down the Selenus coast or heading across the Swirling Seas to find safe harbor in Epan or Ilsal.

There were three inland canals, which acted like the bloodlines of the legion and the rest of Selenus. Carts from other nearby towns, cities, and villages or just trading companies brought their wares with them to sell at Norlund.

The city was bright and refreshing.

"I'll be able to get my final parts." Tommie sat up in his saddle and touched his coin purse. He squeezed it a few more times before he looked around and checked the contents. *I've only got three gold and twenty silver left. I hope it's enough.*

They rode down the hill and into the city. The guards checked their papers and guided them toward a place where they could have their mounts looked after while they were inside Norlund.

"Much nicer here," Anthony said.

"They deal with other races all the time. The traders from Epan and Ilsal are from all of the races. Not many humans come here, but there are a few. Most of them tend to keep to themselves while in Norlund," Aila said.

They found the place to have their mounts looked after.

"Don't you have any coins?" Aila hissed to Anthony.

"Does it look like I have a coin purse just hanging around here?" Anthony muttered back as the stable hand's smile started to turn suspicious.

"Tommie," Anthony called out but Tommie was wandering down the streets, his eyes wide as he rubbed his hands in glee.

Aila's hand rested on Tommie's shoulder. "We're good friends, right? You don't happen to have some money to spare, do you?"

Tommie wanted to escape her grip but she sensed his reaction, her hand holding him like a vise.

"But of course we're good friends. How much might you need?" He smiled brightly as he wailed on the inside. *I worked hard for that gold!*

"A silver and fifty coppers will do." Aila smiled sweetly.

Tommie's smile was all the more forced as he passed over the coinage.

"Thank you! We'll look for a ship out of here tonight." Aila headed back to Anthony.

"How are we going to pay for a ship?" Anthony asked.

"We'll get to that when we get to it. You think that the elves could have given us a little bit of spending money when we were leaving," Aila muttered.

Tommie snuck away and then fled. *I'm free! I'm free! Okay, now I need parts!* Tommie chuckled to himself as he started to wander through the stalls, looking for the different items he might need.

There is a thermal discombobulator and even a heat conversion thinga-whopper! Now I thought that I would need the thinga-whopper, but Anthony did say that the discombobulator would be harder to add in, but then it would last much longer and give me a higher power output.

Tommie paused for a moment and he frowned.

Am I angry at Anthony? I don't think so. Maybe a little hurt that he didn't tell me. Though he probably just forgot to tell me. Tommie shrugged and chuckled. *It is Anthony, after all. I guess that he might not find his head if it wasn't attached. Skeleton jokes! Oh, this is going to be good.* Tommie was laughing in front of the stall.

The vendor looked around at the others; they made eye contact and then shrugged. Who *hadn't* seen a slightly mad gnome engineer? The vendor sighed and rethought his life choices and selling parts to gnomes.

"I would like to take one of your thermal discombobulators!" Tommie smiled at the vendor.

"A fine eye, my young gnome engineer!"

"How could you tell I'm an engineer?"

"I have an eye for these things," the vendor said.

Tommie didn't see the other vendors rolling their eyes.

"I can let it go for seventy gold. It is of the finest quality, made by some of the master gnome engineers in the Ilsal isles!"

***

Aila and Anthony had walked up and down the pier looking for a ship that was heading to Ilsal. There were plenty of them, but the fastest route was to go to Epan, then ride to Sunset Pier and take a boat from there to Ilsal.

The problem was they had no gold and so they had no passage.

"We need to find a way to make some coin still." Anthony sighed.

Aila was chewing on some sweet cane as she looked around the harbor. There were people loading and unloading the boats. An unfortunate crew member tripped; the box that he was carrying went off the pier and into the water.

"I just had an idea," Aila said, looking at the box that the crew member had dropped.

The foreman was yelling at them.

"What's that?" Anthony asked.

He turned as he got a kick to the chest.

"Not Sparta again!" Anthony yelled as he hit the water and started sinking.

"See if you can find anything on the bottom that's useful!" Aila yelled after him.

Anthony was already submerged as she let out a sigh and felt the sun on her skin.

"Some nice peace and quiet." Aila found a place to sit down and got comfortable. "Not as nice as the moonlight, but it does make you sleepy." She got comfortable, ready to wait for the little submerged man to come up with loot.

I wonder what is down there?

***

Aila was sunbathing as a bedazzled set of armor walked out of the water, *covered* in seaweed and stinking of mud. Aila held her nose and used a water blasting spell.

"Blasting off again!" Anthony yelled as he was thrown back into the water.

He came out, muttering to himself, bedecked in different items. He wore jewelry and carried plates and a box of booze.

"Well, look at this haul!" Aila smiled from ear to ear as she pulled a few of the items off Anthony, inspecting them closer.

"Ah, good workmanship. Shame it was at the bottom of the bay. Well, if we can clean these up, then we can get a good price!" Aila started to rub the different jewelry.

"I forgot just how much elves love shiny things—like magpies of the races," Anthony muttered. He shook his leg; rings and a few coins came out. He opened his helmet and reached in, pulling out a slightly rusted candlestick.

"Shinies!" Aila looked as if she were going to break out into a jig as she collected all of the different loot on the ground.

"That should be good," Anthony said.

"Oh, and this one would be perfect with my eyes. Wouldn't this look fine on my finger?" Aila was off in her own world.

"You do know we have to sell them, right?"

"Don't talk about my shinies like that," she hissed at Anthony.

Anthony jumped back, tripped and fell into the water for the *third* time.

Aila gathered up the loot, put it into her pack and headed off to give them some care.

Anthony got out of the water, not seeing any sign of Aila.

He got to the top of the stairs and he looked around.

***

Anthony went and retrieved Ramona and her two young ones. He hung out with them, playing with them and watching them paddle in the water happily.

Aila and Tommie appeared some time later. Tommie looked dirtier than before and he was patting his pack that was on his front with glee, even if his legs were having trouble keeping the weight of whatever was in his pack up.

Aila wore fine new robes, turning people's eyes as she passed like a regal queen.

"Okay, so how much do we have for passage?" Anthony asked, looking at the finest ship. It was an elegant passenger vessel with gold-encrusted crenellations on it. They even had feather beds aboard and boasted a full fresh menu, as well as a security escort with magical formations on the side of the ship. She looked as if she could dominate the seas.

"I was able to get this robe on sale. It came with a complete set. Isn't it *gorgeous*?" Aila asked.

"It's colorful and shiny. Are those enchantments?" Anthony staggered backward. He had enchanted armor; he knew just how expensive wearable enchanted items could be.

"I knew you had an eye for detail. These magical enchantments will allow me much greater control over my mana. I really was listening to you when you were talking about spell casting. See, I want to follow in your footsteps and I can only think of doing that with this robe."

"How much was it?" Anthony asked in a pained voice.

"Well, it was a good deal, as I saw it—a real bargain. Though I lost the shinies. We can always get more, right!" Aila laughed and smiled, as she half lifted her foot.

Anthony swiftly retreated out of her range. "How much do you have left?" he yelled, now at a safe enough distance.

"I've still got thirty coppers left. See, it's a really good deal, no?"

"I scraped the bottom of the bay for all of that! Why did you think I was so muddy and covered in seaweed?" Anthony cried, holding his head.

Aila had an awkward smile on her face. "I'm sure that you can find more."

Anthony's eyes fell on the passenger ship, seeing the refined folk who were being guided up to the ship, then back to the ecstatic gnome and unabashed elf who was gathering attention with her new robes.

Anthony's eyes moved down the row of boats, from the newer and well-cared-for behemoths down to the cargo ships. They were no less smaller but their uses were purely utilitarian.

Anthony started down in that direction.

"Where are you going?" Aila asked.

"To find a boat!" Anthony yelled.

He went to the different vessels, going through three boat crews before he walked up to a surly-looking shark kin captain. "What is the biggest problem that you have and will fixing it get me and my friends passage to Epan?" Anthony asked.

The captain looked over Anthony, then Tommie and Aila. "Don't you have the gold?" the captain asked in a low voice.

"I *did*. The *elf* spent it." Anthony sighed.

"Ahh." The shark kin captain nodded in understanding. "Well, there is one thing. The city has got this big 'berg that has been blocking up the sewers, calling all kinds of troubles. My missus and the kids haven't been able to use the toilets in a week. If you can clear out the 'berg, then it'll get you passage."

"Consider it done!" Anthony said. "Where is it?"

"Go to the Old Hog. Two streets down, toward the wall—that's where I heard it was last." The captain nodded.

Chapter: The 'Berg Incident

"Wait here." Anthony stepped into the sewers. They all had night vision, but in tight, confined spaces, Aila wouldn't be of much help and she was still protective of her new attire. Tommie was a good engineer but he wasn't a fighter and the water would have been up to his chest while it was up to Anthony's thighs. Also, it was a sewer; it was pretty easy to get all kinds of infections and being an undead, Anthony was probably not going to be killed by a bunch of bacteria.

"Gross," Anthony muttered as he walked through the sewer.

He saw something blocking it up ahead, as well as heard slurping noises.

"Huh?" Anthony said.

A face appeared on the collection of items, looking at Anthony.

"It's a sewer golem!" Anthony yelled out.

The sewer golem seemed a bit displeased. It let out a yell, hurling sewage at Anthony.

"Will you stop that!" Anthony yelled. He waded forward, drawing his sword and deflecting the incoming long-range attacks.

He closed with the 'berg golem but it let out a snarl and jumped forward, startling Anthony as he put in too much strength.

The 'berg exploded into a mist. A green haze surrounded Anthony.

"Ugh! I'll never get the smell out!" Anthony yelled.

He was cleaning himself off as he saw the power core of the golem. "With this, I can increase my mana!" He reached forward as he heard Tommie and Aila talking.

I should probably let them know I'm...is that a flame?

"N—"

***

"What was that?" Tommie asked.

162

"I'm not sure." Aila used her flame spell. Her flame was torn away from her hand and a light flashed before their eyes as an explosion went off closer to the dockyards. A geyser of water and bits of the 'berg were catapulted out of the sewers with a cartwheeling and screaming knight.

Aila and Tommie looked at each other, then looked around, edging away from the sewer grate and making sure no one saw them as they took off at a run.

Chapter: Across The Swirling Seas

Anthony had gained them passage aboard the mighty *Hubberston*. He consumed a mana core, which had increased his overall mana capacity once again. He'd rid the city of Norlund of a monster sewage 'berg, gaining the admiration of the people.

But he was also thrown clear across the Norlund bay, taking him three hours to walk under the bay and requiring three more washes with soap to get rid of the remaining scent from the 'berg.

Captain Lothir kept his word and took them aboard, setting off the next morning.

Tommie had retreated to the bowels of the ship to play with his new parts. Anthony was sitting on the quarterdeck, playing a game of cards with the captain and some of the crew.

The sweet sounds of seasickness came from the rear.

Aila didn't seem to be the biggest fan of ships. At least her stomach wasn't, though Anthony had thoughtfully secured her to the rear of the ship with rope to make sure that she wouldn't fall overboard.

"Something feels wrong," Aila said.

"Sounds like it too," Anthony quipped.

"No, the mana is getting stirred up," Aila said.

"Mana storm?" one of the crew members said.

"Shouldn't be," Captain Lothir said.

"We've got mana gathering off the port bow!" the man on watch called out.

"Dammit!" Lothir yelled and rang the bell next to the steering wheel. "Mana storm! Make sure the gear is secured and unfurl the sails!"

People who had been taking a rest below decks now rushed out with pale expressions as they ran up the rigging to loosen the sails.

Anthony jumped up the rigging as well, letting loose the sails; they snapped in the wind. Lothir turned the ship, catching the wind, propelling them away from the mana storm.

"It looks to be coming closer, Cap!" the watcher said. "The water is glowing!"

The clouds seemed to roll in on them and the skies darkened. A vortex of water and mana stirred up, connecting the waters to the skies.

The ship was jostled by the wind. A man screamed out as he lost his positioning.

"Come on, fella!" Anthony yelled, grabbing a rope and jumping. As he swung in an arc, wings appeared on his back. He grabbed the man and circled back around, landing on the boat.

"Y-you?" Lothir needed a second to find his words. "Are you the winged Guardian Anthony?"

"You heard of me?" Anthony asked. *Well, this is going to be awkward if people connect me to the 'berg incident.*

"I know some of the traders who go down there. They told us about a person with golden wings who protected the city."

"Yeah, they're pretty sweet." Anthony looked over at the water that was slowly rising up.

Black, almost green, waves appeared, thrashing together and lifting up from the water, suspended in the air to form a turbid sphere.

They rested there, drawing in an incredible amount of mana that shot into the sphere of waves.

Tommie ran up on the deck as the sailors dropped down from the rigging. The sails unfurled as they tried to flee.

"Anthony, is that an elemental?" Tommie's voice climbed in volume as he pointed at the glowing water creature that seemed to be made of sea waves.

"What did I tell you?"

"If it makes you puckered up, scared, and nature seems like it's broken, then it is probably an elemental!"

"Good, Tommie—you were listening." Anthony strode forward and patted

him on the shoulder.

"Now, you should all probably get below decks. It's nothing to panic about! Just don't need the screaming and running around—distracts from some totally awesome sailing!" Anthony said.

Tommie and the rest of the sailors looked at Anthony as Aila threw up over the side of the boat.

"How *do* you have anything left in there?" Anthony asked, genuinely surprised.

"How is that the most alarming thing, when there is a water elemental off our bow and where did you get that hat?" Tommie looked at the pirate hat that was on top of Anthony's helmet at a jaunty angle.

"Pretty dashing—" The wind pulled on Anthony's hat, and he clamped it down. "That's it, sea elemental—you're going down!"

The elemental seemed to hear. The sphere expanded and the waves turned into a black and green whale with eyes that glowed brighter than blue gems.

The whale dropped from the sky and it let out a roar that flattened the water around with force. It hit the stilled water and sent up massive waves that rippled out in every direction.

"Lothir, get your people below decks!" Anthony yelled. The clouds above shook with thunder and lightning as rain poured down.

"I only just met you!" Lothir yelled.

"I'm a guardian angel, buddy, but I can't save anyone who falls off the boat. You're welcome to stay, but tie yourself in!" Anthony yelled.

"You gone up against an elemental before?" Lothir yelled.

"A few!" Anthony laughed.

Lothir looked from Anthony to the wheel before he nodded.

Anthony took the wheel, turning them toward the elemental.

"Everyone who's not essential, get below decks—it's time to ride!" Anthony grabbed onto the steering wheel with one hand and held his hat with the other. Power flowed from him into the ship. Their speed lurched, the boat rearing up before it charged forward with greater speed than before.

Lothir tied himself in as a few others gritted their teeth and made sure that they were tied in as well.

"Solomon, you're on lookout. Dave, give us some more speed! Bruce, buff the ship!"

The rain came in sideways now and people listened to what Anthony said.

"Aila, what are you doing out here still?" Anthony asked as they were all cleared away.

"I'm still tied to the banister! Untie me!"

Anthony looked back and into the storm and the waves that were coming at them. "No can do! Don't worry—I have trust in the knots!"

"Is this about the robes?" Aila yelled.

"Sorry, I can't hear you!" Anthony shared a look with Lothir.

"We should trim the sails!" he yelled.

"We're going to need the speed to get up those waves!" Anthony said.

The waves were now towering above them.

Lothir looked at them and shivered. "What's the plan?"

"We do some surfing, cargo-ship style," Anthony said.

"What is surfing?"

"It's a really fun sport in Ilsal."

"The one where they use flimsy wood to ride down waves, can hit rocks or drown from the waves crashing down on them?" Lothir's voice changed.

"You really know how to highlight the negative points, don't you?" Anthony frowned.

He looked back at the ship. It had transformed. The five masts had black flames that couldn't be extinguished by the torrential downpour.

The ship was glowing green and gold, with Dave's head as the ship's figurehead; his wings jutted out from either side of the ship

"Here we go!" Anthony yelled.

Dave put all of his strength into it; their speed increased again as they reached the bottom of the wave.

"Get ready to pull the sails in and then release them!" Anthony yelled.

The crew had grim faces as they worked on the rigging, preparing the sails.

Anthony grinned inside his helmet. *This is the coolest! Wait till I tell Claire!*

"Bring the sails in!" Anthony yelled.

They hauled on the ropes, bringing the sails up. Dave kept their momentum up as they climbed the wave.

"Hold on to something!" Anthony yelled, holding onto his hat as everyone clung to different parts of the ship.

Anthony felt the motion of the ship, the wind acting on it, the pull of the water underneath, their momentum declining even as Dave strained. Just as they were about to start going backward, Anthony cut the wheel to the side, turning it with all of his might. As the rudder cut against the water, the boat creaked and groaned with the forces trying to tear it apart. Bruce's glow intensified.

They shifted and then turned.

"Come on, you beauty. Don't fail us now, *Hubberston*!" Lothir yelled.

"Dave, now!"

Dave had stopped flapping his wings and now put them out to the side, catching the wave. They started to fall down the side of the wave, gathering momentum.

Anthony felt the bite, the power and the speed.

Dave used his other wing, pushing them into the wave as Anthony used the rudder. They carved through the massive wave, curving around it.

"Yelling Atoll, here we come! Ready to release on those sails, lads?"

"Ready!" The crew replied, looking at him with eyes filled with anxiousness and a little bit of hope.

"All right then, on my command!" Anthony laughed as he felt the wind against his armor and the spray of the sea water as they surfed the massive tsunami wave.

Their speed increased as they angled down more. They were now like a boat out of hell as the *Hubberston* creaked and complained but remained together. The cargo-designed boat was much hardier and larger than passenger ships.

And right now she was the most beautiful ship that Anthony had ever laid eyes on.

"Foresails!" Anthony yelled as he cut the rudder. They turned, no longer cutting along the wave but now plunging down it as they picked up speed.

Anthony let out a whoop and he held onto his hat.

The others were all screaming as they moved faster than old *Hubberston* had ever gone before. Dave flapped his wings eagerly; their speed increased to the point that they were lifted up out of the water, gliding on just Dave's wings, before they skipped across the water.

"Release the sails!" Anthony boomed.

The towering waves were still behind them as Dave flapped his wings as fast as possible. They shot across the water, the wind at their backs as concussive waves of force rolled forward.

The sails dropped, snapping out to full sail as they surged ahead.

"That's it, girl!" Anthony barked and patted the wheel as they shot across the Swirling Seas, the wind at their back and the thrill of surviving rushing through their veins.

The crew cheered but didn't let go as the speed was still astronomical.

***

The crew of the *Serendipity* was just serving dinner to their passengers. They had seen the mana storm from the top of their rigging but it was far enough away to not affect them.

They had continued on their course; the captain was called up to the quarterdeck as he was seeing the guests. He excused himself and went to the quarterdeck.

"What is it?"

His first mate passed him the telescope. He extended it and looked out at where he was pointing.

There was a ship that had green lightning running across the ship. Golden wings were flapping along its side and it was wreathed in black flames.

The hellish ship shot across the water faster than any ship that he had seen before.

It shot past the aft of the ship, coming in the direction of the mana storm.

"What in the hells?" the captain asked as it shot past. He caught a glimpse of the captain: a man wearing full armor, holding onto his hat with one hand, steering with his leg and waving with his free hand.

The crew were all moving around the deck slowly and there was a person tied down to the rear of the ship. As fast as it arrived, it passed, continuing on its path.

"Was that a cargo ship?" someone asked.

"Cursed ship raised from Davy Jones's Locker," another said in fear.

"Not a word of this to the guests. Cut our course away from that mana storm. We don't need to run into trouble. We'll sail all night." The captain snapped the telescope closed.

Chapter: Yelling Atoll

The *Hubberston* slowed down after half a day. Dave, Bruce, and Solomon returned to Anthony, who passed the hat back to Lothir.

"Will you untie me!" Aila complained.

"Coming, coming." Anthony undid the bindings and Aila stood up.

"No!" Her legs failed her and she grabbed onto the railing to support her.

"Urgh, pins and needles...the *worst*," Anthony said.

"How could you leave me on the back for that!" Aila yelled.

"How could you make me go into the sewer and fight a 'berg?" Anthony muttered to himself but she could hear him.

She looked at him with thinned eyes before she reached out a hand. "Truce?"

"For now," Anthony said.

A chill ran through Aila.

They continued their journey over the next few days. Tommie and a few of the engineering types were in and out of the hold the entire time.

Anthony and the sailors bonded while Aila finished with her seasickness and admired her new clothes.

They came into the port of Yelling Atoll. It was a natural port with a series of caves to the south. It was a large port but there were only a few ships there and less of a city. Most people seemed to just gather items and then head off to the other cities of Epan.

"Is there something wrong with Yelling Atoll?" Aila asked Lothir.

"You'll find out soon enough," Lothir said.

"They look a bit upset." Aila went over to where Anthony was leaning against a railing.

"Well, it *is* Yelling Atoll," Anthony said.

"You saved their lives, though. Shouldn't they be a bit happier seeing land?" Aila asked.

"You'll see soon enough," Anthony said.

"What do you mean?" Aila asked, getting annoyed with this mysteriousness. Although the city was small, the land around it was nice and it was warm as well. It looked rather idyllic.

They said their good-byes to the crew and headed off, taking Ramona and her two twins with them. They were all much happier to be on land.

Tommie wobbled as he stepped onto land. "This is going to take some time to readjust to."

Aila was getting nauseous all over again. "What is happening?"

"Oh, well, you could be land sick, though that's pretty rare," Anthony said.

"Land sick?" Aila yelled.

"Yeah, you get used to being on the sea and then you feel weird on the land without the swaying," Anthony said. "Come on, let's get a hotel. We'll use the rest of our coins there and head out in the morning."

"Would you like some cotton?" a man asked in a strange voice.

"What was that?" Tommie asked.

"Cotton." The man held up some cotton buds.

Anthony moved his hands to talk to the man; he nodded and smiled, replying with hand gestures as well.

Anthony and the man waved to each other and the man kept going.

"What was that?" Aila asked.

"Sign language. What...hmm, well, I guess you technically did grow up under a lot of rocks." Anthony shrugged and kept going.

They found an inn on the outside of town, making sure that Ramona and her children were well taken care of so that they would be ready for the journey the next day.

"This place is beautiful." Tommie looked out over the bay and the rocks, and felt the warm breeze.

"I know, but everyone seems to think that."

"Ahh!"

"What was that?" Tommie jumped as a terrifying scream filled the air.

"AHHH! Noo!!! Ahh!"

"That'd be the Yelling Atoll!" someone said, stuffing cotton into their ears.

"It actually yells?" Aila yelled.

They went to find Anthony, who was reading a book.

"The Yelling Atoll actually yells?"

"Yeah, those caves we saw coming in—the wind goes through there and makes noises. Bit freaky—hard to sleep with, really. The port is good and cheaper because of it. Most of the people in the town are actually deaf."

"That's why you used sign language!" Aila snapped her fingers.

Anthony snapped his back and pointed a finger pistol at her. "Bingo!"

***

Tommie suffered through the night, working on his Gnome-inator plans. Anthony tended to Ramona and her children, using earmuffs to keep out the noise.

As soon as they were able to, Aila and Tommie grabbed their gear and headed down to the stables, mounting up.

It was a few hours before they left the screaming and yelling behind.

"So, what did you think of Yelling Atoll?" Anthony laughed.

"Like, it's a *nice* city but I don't think it was everything that it was supposed to be," Tommie said.

"The yelling make it impossible to sleep?"

"Yup! Creepy as hell after a few hours!" Tommie tightened the last strap on his bag before he clambered up his mount.

"Well, you know, you shouldn't believe all the hype. If your expectations are too high, they just get shot down. Achieve high, aim low—that is the past, young one," Anthony said, like an age-old sage.

"Do you know what he's saying?" Tommie asked Aila.

"Oh, I stopped listening after I woke him up." Aila shrugged. "Maintained my sanity that way."

Tommie nodded at her sage advice.

"No respect for elders," Anthony muttered.

Chapter: Final Component

They travelled north and passed a few small villages. The island of Epan was made up of mostly sailors. Inland, there weren't many people; those who moved inland raised cattle and crops.

The people were easy and carefree; the wars of the humans and the beast kin were far away and the Epan navy worked hand-in-hand with the Ilsal navy to clear away pirates and make sure that no one threatened their lands.

The other countries all had their own navy force but the Islanders' force was much stronger. They worked with people from all of the races, fighting together and strengthening each other.

As they went north, the trio reached the three sister cities. They ran across the neck of Epan. To the east was Sunrise Harbor. In the middle was Tamar, the capital of Epan. And to the west there was Sunset Pier. Canals ran between the two ports and trade was booming. In a place with so many different races, including gnomes, Tommie was excited to find the last few remaining parts.

They went to Sunset Pier. The three cities were basically one large city with three regions. When they got to the city, they still didn't have enough money to get a ride north. Tommie didn't have the funds to get his parts, either.

"Once more into the depths." Anthony sighed and jumped into the bay, wading around for a few hours before he returned with different random objects.

He gave a few to Tommie and then took the rest with him to a jewelers, dragging Aila along, who pouted the entire time.

Tommie wandered the markets as he searched for the final part.

"A rotating gimbaled power mount." Tommie's eyes glowed as his face was pressed up against the glass, looking at the object in the center of the display case.

He burst into the shop and went up to the counter. "Power mount! Gimbal, money, need!" Tommie looked up at the human at the counter, who raised an eyebrow but seemed numb to the crazed gnome.

"Rotating gimbalized power mount?" he asked.

Tommie nodded.

"That will be fourteen gold," the man said.

Tommie dumped out his items on the table.

"Up for a barter?" Tommie grinned.

The man looked at him a bit differently now as he looked at the gem-encrusted items.

He took out a few tools as Tommie tapped his foot.

He was a trader only because he was looking for parts he needed for his Gnome-inator. He was a cutthroat negotiator, but when it came to something that was related to his dreams, he was impulsive and money was no longer an issue.

The man finished examining the items and pushed some back. "I have your rotating gimbalized power mount." He went around the counter and up to the display. There were four guards with him, all powerful existences, watching to make sure that someone wouldn't try their luck.

The man at the counter undid different defensive measures to get to the rotating gimbalized power mount.

Do they think a dragon is going to try to raid their store with powerful formations like that? Tommie had wondered how they could easily display such treasures in their front window. Now, seeing their defenses, he understood that anyone would be a fool to try to steal from the store.

The man took the rotating gimbalized power mount back behind the counter and packaged it up. He placed the box in front of Tommie.

He let out an excited noise as the other engineers in the store looked at him with jealousy.

"With this, it will be complete!" Tommie cackled and ran toward the door.

The door opened, smacking Tommie in the face.

He bounced back up again as if nothing had happened and ran past the hobgoblins and their goblin charges.

"I am not selling you any more boom contraptions!" The man at the counter, who had been impassive before, even with so much gold on the line, was now filled with energy and his face paled in fear.

"We just came to browse and show the little ones around."

"No! No!" the store manager said, his world crumbling around him as the little goblins looked around in wide-eyed curiosity, eyeing complex mechanical parts and systems as if they were their new favorite toy.

Tommie was making tracks down the street, covering the distance quickly. He saw Anthony and Aila looking around. Aila was pouting and petting her mount, complaining to them as they looked bored from it all.

Tommie's mount was bugging Ramona. Anthony looked around, spotting Tommie; he waved his hand and started up a gangway.

Tommie ran up the gangway and grabbed his mount, helping pull them onto the ship.

"He's with us," Anthony said.

"Do you have a large open room?" Tommie asked, butting in.

"We have a few free, but they'll cost more," the beast kin said.

"Ten silver for the trip!" Anthony interjected. He must have seen the crazed look on Tommie's face as he reached into his vest.

"Fifteen, with another five deposit for damages," the beast kin said. "He has that engineering look in his eyes."

Anthony paused and looked at Tommie before passing over the silvers.

"This way, my engineering companion." The beast kin man led Tommie onto the ship and then down into its hold.

Fifty coppers got some help moving the different cloth-covered parts off Tommie's mount and into the spare room that was a half-filled cargo hold.

Tommie set to work, checking on his different parts as the beast kin shook his head and went above deck.

Tommie worked day and night as they travelled along the Epan coast and crossed the Golden Channel.

Morning was just arriving as Tommie looked at his masterpiece. He took the rotating gimbalized power mount and placed it into the contraption. He had to get out a hammer and tap it into place a few times.

He locked it into place and looked at the contraption.

"The Gnome-inator," Tommie said, admiring the wonky-looking machine.

He activated a few different buttons and levers.

The machine burbled and then faltered.

Tommie took his wrench and smacked the Gnome-inator. It took a few more coaxing hits before it burbled again and then its core fired up the rotating gimbaled power mount starting to rotate slowly and then speeding up so that the arms around the crystalline heart of the gnominator couldn't be seen.

"It lives! It lives!" Tommie laughed, out of fatigue and madness, finally seeing his completed dream. He hugged his masterpiece, feeling the cold metal vibrating with power.

"The power is connected and functioning how it should be, I still need to get it calibrated and adjust the subsystems," Tommie said.

"El Sai ahead!" the sailor on watch yelled.

People started to wake up across the ship as they got ready to make landfall.

Tommie looked over to the large wooden crates to the side of his room.

"Dammit!" He pulled the boxes over and groaned in complaint. He quickly started to dismantle the gnominator for transport.

**

El Sai looked like a city that had been built by all of the races.

The port had different docks and multiple shipyards. The port jutted out like a half moon, with signs of expansion along the edges. At the back of the ports, there were some flat lands before it ran into a mountain range.

The mountain range had been turned into a city with different homes jutting out of it. One could see elvish tree homes that dotted the mountain. On different rock outcroppings, there were a mishmash of different homes and buildings in different styles. Instead of looking chaotic, it created a strange harmony, with one's eyes being drawn in every direction.

The dominating combined fleet patrolled the waters. Defenses were built into the mountain, with towers that jutted out of the harbor, crewed with the Ilsal navy.

Ilsal was a land made by all of the races. Even with everyone together, they only grew in strength. They were known as the land of academics. They had technology, universities, animal raising industries, and more.

"You know that the beast kin and the humans are both pressuring Ilsal to join their side, to supply them with weapons?" Aila said.

"I'm guessing they said no?" Anthony asked.

"They disagreed but the humans and beast kin were vindictive—they planted spies in Ilsal. They were going to take them by force. When they attacked the different manufacturing shops, they found out that it was a trap. Ilsal trapped the spies and tracked down their accomplices before moving their fleets to face Selenus and Radal. They didn't dare to say anything. The humans and beast kin didn't know what was true or not." Aila laughed.

"How were they able to root out the spies?"

"They used their police force and judiciary system. Their political system and judiciary system are their main pillars of strength. They have schools for judges and for lawyers." Aila looked at Anthony.

"I wonder who started that." Anthony tapped his helmeted chin.

Chapter: Meeting The Chief Justice Of Ilsal

Claire was looking over documents as a middle-aged woman with a refined air walked into the room. She looked like the kind of person that others obeyed.

"My lady," the woman said, showing none of that authority as she bowed to Claire.

"I told you that you can just call me Claire."

"I am just giving respect due to the position," the woman said with a level smile.

Claire looked up, her eyes thinning at the woman who merely smiled with mischief.

Claire sighed to hide her amusement as she sat up fully. "You know the three that the elves said would be visiting us—the dark elf, the knight with a tree on the back of his armor, and a gnome?"

"Yes, my lady." The woman turned serious, as if receiving her marching orders.

"They have arrived in El Sai. The elven embassy has probably sent out people to meet with them. Be ready to receive them," Claire said.

"Do you wish to meet with them?"

Claire pressed her lips together and then looked at her hand. A flash of pain appeared in her eyes and she felt a hint of fear—an unfamiliar feeling to her—as she closed her fist.

"No," Claire said.

"Very well."

"See what their plans are, and..." Claire reached into her desk and pulled out a necklace.

She opened it. Inside, there were two vivid photos that hadn't aged with time. There was one of a woman who was looking past the painting, her face filled with joy and mirth. The other was a man with flowing brown hair, hugging the woman from behind, as if he would never let her go; the woman was trying to struggle free playfully but one could see the way their two eyes met. They never wanted to be anywhere but in each other's arms.

Claire closed the locket and then held it out.

The lady took it.

"Make sure that he gets that, Tamarra," Claire said.

***

Aila's hands dropped to her daggers as three people seemed to materialize out of an alleyway.

"You really need to work on your detection skills. What's up, boys and lady?" Anthony waved to the people.

One pulled his hood back, revealing his high elf appearance.

"It is good to see you, Guardian Anthony. We are due for an appointment with the chief justice. Would you care to join?"

"Sure. I wouldn't mind meeting the person who set this all up," Anthony said.

Aila stored her blades away as they went through the city. They reached a large building, where people were wearing funky white hats, others wearing blue ones.

Tommie was fidgety, patting his cloth-covered pieces on his mount's back.

They passed the guards without too much trouble.

"I'll wait with the mounts!" Tommie volunteered before they could say anything.

"Okay," Aila said, looking at Tommie and then his cloth bags in interest.

Aila and Anthony followed the leading elf who had talked to them and the guards.

"Is something wrong?" Aila asked Anthony, feeling that something was off.

"I'm not sure." Anthony sounded confused.

They were led into a room where a woman worked on reports. She looked up from her work and her eyes cleared as she took the glasses off her nose. She was a human with a dark complexion.

The elf bowed to her respectfully. "Chief Justice, thank you for agreeing to see us." The elf then rose. "I will allow you to speak in private."

"Thank you, Ambassador Ryuil." The chief justice nodded to the elf, who quickly left.

Aila and Anthony were left in the room with her. The doors locked and an enchantment activated, cutting them off from the outside world.

***

"Guardian Anthony, it is good to see you. I have heard about the Guardians of the past," the woman said, her severe expression turning into a smile.

"So you know something of the past?" Anthony's heart shifted in his chest, as if he needed to do something but he didn't know what.

"We have more complete records here. Most of the fighting was on the mainland, after all," she said.

"What about the forces of chaos that are active now?"

"We have been gathering information. The courts on Ilsal have made sure that chaos doesn't set in here. Agents of Chaos have tried repeatedly. We have an ongoing program with Epan, who have secured themselves from Agents of Chaos, while there are Agents of Chaos to be found all across Radal and Selenus. The Deepwood has been hard to infiltrate. With the elves' high sensitivity toward mana, they can sense the Agents of Chaos with a higher degree of accuracy.

"As people go deeper into the woods, then the elves with more mana will be able to find Agents of Chaos faster. With their clan system and strict rules, it's hard to infiltrate. Though it has cut them off from the humans and beast kin, they still go to Epan and Ilsal regularly."

Anthony nodded.

Aila stood there, listening and trying to learn.

Tamarra tapped her desk. "Ah, I have something for you." Tamarra pulled out a small box and brought it around her desk, holding it out to Anthony.

Anthony took the box and his heart tightened.

Where are you? Anthony used the Eyes of Truth. He saw through the walls of the building and saw a hidden entrance in the shelves behind the desk.

His heart was still tightening as Anthony felt compelled to go through that hidden entrance.

"Anthony?" Aila asked as Anthony walked forward, as if a puppet with someone else pulling on his strings.

***

Claire was watching Tamarra's office. When she saw her pass the box to Anthony, she had to look away. She cut off the transmission and sat back in her chair, feeling all of her years.

She felt the pain, deep in her bones.

He's so close, but if he was to see me in this state... She would have cried out if she could, thrown a tantrum if she released her self-control.

She felt something; she looked up. She heard something being broken in the distance. Alarms were going off.

She got up from her desk and moved to the main hall. She saw Damien in his full armor standing at the entrance, guarding her with his massive aged war hammer.

"Huh? Not again!" Damien complained as he was thrown to the side as if he were a rag doll.

There's only one person I know who can throw Damien like that!

Claire felt giddy as she saw that familiar armor standing at the entrance to the hall. Behind him, Tamarra and Aila ran up.

Neither of them said anything. The hall was silent, other than Damien falling out of the wall and crashing to the floor.

***

Anthony's heart moved in all different kinds of ways as he looked at the woman in front of him.

She was a lich: an embodiment of evil, someone who had destroyed their humanity. Though Anthony didn't feel revulsion. He felt as if he were burning all over; he felt as if he were on needles and wrapped in pillows.

His eyes burned brighter than ever as parts of his memories started to fall into place. It was as if he had been trying to solve a puzzle without a picture, but now it came into focus.

A young knight who had wandered, helping people until he ran into a young mage who was aloof from all of the world. Who seemed untouchable. They didn't realize that they had fallen for each other as they went to join the Guardian Academy to help others. They had denied their thoughts, their emotions until they graduated and were put on assignment together.

Anthony remembered that mysterious smile on their mentor's face as they were sent off on their first assignment.

All of those emotions, those beautiful and precious memories, rolled forward into one word.

"Claire," Anthony said.

"Anthony," Claire said.

Anthony pulled off his helmet and dropped it on the ground. "I'm home."

Claire let out a laugh. It was broken and painful to hear from her dried-up body. To Anthony, he was soaring as he walked toward her.

"Do you know why?" Anthony asked as he advanced.

"Why?" Claire cocked her hip and tapped her lip.

He saw a young girl with a playful smile on her face as she seemed to be looking for the answer herself.

Anthony walked up to her and pulled her gently to his armor, being as gentle as possible as some of her clothes and skin flaked off. He leaned down so his mouth was next to hers. *Her* heart inside his chest beat rapidly, as if a nervous schoolgirl.

"You're my home."

Claire shook as she put her arms around Anthony.

She tried to speak out, to tell him her loneliness, to tell him how she had missed him.

Anthony didn't need to hear it. Holding her, it was as if two parts of a whole connected.

Behind him, Dave appeared. Solomon had a smiling mask and Bruce crossed his arms and nodded.

***

Aila looked at the skeleton and the lich hugging, confused. She still held onto her blades. The knight who had been planted in the wall came over, as dust fell from his armor.

"Protector Damien," Tamarra said with an awkward look.

"Hey, little T," Damien said.

"You look different," Anthony said.

"What does that mean?" Claire pushed back and looked at him.

"Nothing that a little moisturizer wouldn't fix," Anthony joked.

"You!" Claire had black flames around her and Anthony started running.

"I was joking!" Anthony said with a little panic, looking at his familiars, who looked around, examining the walls and the ceiling, leaving Anthony to fend for himself as purple and black fire balls shot out at him.

A squeak escaped his face as he dodged it.

"Babe! Honey!" Three more went at his head and he power slid on the floor.

"Clair-ikins!" he yelled as he did cartwheels.

"A little moisturizer! You don't think I've tried!" Claire yelled.

"They'll be at this for a while." Damien took off his helmet and revealed his handsome face.

But Aila could feel the necromantic power rolling off him. *Is he undead?*

"Tea?" Damien offered, waving them over to a side room as Anthony pleaded with Claire.

"I waited for you for *five hundred years*! Anyone would be haggard after knowing you for just five minutes!" Claire yelled.

"Babe! Babe! Come on, we can talk about this!" Anthony cried out as Claire stopped hurling fireballs. "Your beauty only grows with time! You are a goddess in my eyes." Anthony piled on the compliments.

Claire let out a terrible laugh as more fireballs filled the air.

"What did I say wrong now?" Anthony whined. He was hit with several fireballs, which launched him backward into a wall, hitting him repeatedly and creating a tunnel in the hall's side.

"Ah, young love." Damien smiled.

Aila lowered her daggers in defeat as she followed him into the kitchen.

"Safer to leave them to it, I think, and Damien's scones are *amazing*." Tamarra smiled like a little girl.

How is this my life now? Aila thought to herself, looking up. But no gods answered her.

Please, if you have some time, leave a review or rating, they help to spread the word about the book!

You can check out my other books, what I'm working on and upcoming releases through the following means:

Website: http://michaelchatfield.com/
Twitter: @chatfieldsbooks[1]
Facebook: Michael Chatfield[2]
Goodreads: Goodreads.com/michaelchatfield[3]
Patreon: https://www.patreon.com/michaelchatfieldwrites
Thanks again for reading! ☺

---

1.   https://twitter.com/chatfieldsbooks

2.   https://www.facebook.com/michaelchatfieldsbooks/?ref=hl

3.   https://www.goodreads.com/author/show/14055550.Michael_Chatfield

Made in the USA
Columbia, SC
31 January 2022